Piercing The Veil

KALYNN APPLEWHITE

CHAPTER

1

AN UNRULY GALE HAMMERED against the rooftops of New York, flooding its gutters and eventually its streets as well. The mounds of tarnished snow that had lingered so long in the city's periphery were washed away as the storm ushered in a violent prelude to the coming spring. All fortunate souls had long found shelter. Even the city's menagerie of strays and pests had nested under pavilions and porches to wait out the deluge. Only a few lonely cars traversed the waterway avenues. One such vessel came to a stop outside the unassuming townhouse office numbered 321 Warren Street.

Laura Bennett opened the car door herself, as it was apparent that the driver was in no mood to stand on ceremony if it meant stepping out of the cover of his vehicle. She fumbled desperately with her umbrella as the rain soaked through the sleeves of her woolen jacket. At last, it struggled reluctantly into place, and Laura emerged from the cab. Her first steps soaked through her shoes and stockings. Still, Laura rushed off the flooded street toward the steps. She sighed with great relief as she reached the shelter of the stoop and shut her umbrella, shaking out the moisture. Somehow, despite its protection, her blonde hair had become damp, a few strands clinging to her cheeks.

Lightning illuminated the sky overhead, but she was inside before the sound of thunder followed. The townhouse was home to two stately apartments on either side of the tiled hall, numbered 319 and 320. Judging from outside appearances, they were certainly far grander than the tiny apartment she kept on the West Side, and Laura had always considered herself fairly lucky to have even that. At least it was clean, which was more than could be said for most of the city's housing.

Laura rested her umbrella in the corner beside the door and glanced up the stairs. A green tinted lamp provided a dim light, illuminating the door marked number 321. She supposed it was a rather unassuming door, tucked away in its shadowy corner. It would have hardly registered in her attention if she had not been especially looking for it. But considering what lay beyond, Laura supposed this particular door might just prefer to remain that way. Bolstering her courage with a bracing breath, she began to climb the steps, having come much too far to turn back now.

All morning, she had debated whether to brave the storm in order to keep her appointment. Even minutes before she left her apartment, Laura had convinced herself to stay home. Yet as she glanced at the bed beside her own, the floral sheets perfectly made, creaseless and cold, something had come over her. Laura had gathered her things in a mad rush and charged the streets to find one of the only willing cabs in the entire city to bring her here. Though now, as she stood before the door marked 321, her sense of urgency had drained, leaving her damp and rather cold, wondering if this had all been a mistake. Grief was a rather strange beast indeed, coming and going as it pleased, so often making one do the most peculiar things without explanation or apology.

Her hand felt rather leaden as she raised it to rap softly on the door. Laura waited, the water seeping through her woolen coat to dampen the shoulders of the blouse beneath. Before her, the door opened generously. Camila's familiar features smiled at her from the other side. Her black hair was swept up as elegantly as ever. The dark purple of her skirt was an intriguing compliment to the warm tones of her skin. The kind smile widened on her lips as she waved Laura inside.

"It's good to see you. I had so hoped the weather wouldn't keep you away," Camila said. "Please come in and hang your coat. You're nearly soaked to the bone!"

Laura gave a sheepish laugh as she stepped inside. The light was dim as heavy purple curtains covered the windows. A large bookcase dominated half of the room, stacked with many books and trinket boxes. Beside it, a record player sat idly on an old sewing table. In the center was a circular table with seating for four. A large wardrobe loomed behind it where three stuffed crows perched, surveying the room. Rounding the table was an unfamiliar young woman who could only be the Ms. Maggie Barlow whom Camila had spoken of.

"I'm so glad you were able to make it," Maggie said as Laura hung her coat.

"It is quite a storm," Laura allowed.

Maggie's skin was far fairer than Camila's. Though her hair was done up in a similar fashion, it was a rich brown and held a more natural curl. Laura found herself rather surprised by how ordinary the medium seemed, how like herself. They couldn't be far removed in age, and yet the way Camila had spoken about her gifts…

"I was so sorry to hear about what happened," Camila said, pulling her into a friendly hug. "The whole congregation was, of course. Kathy was such a dear friend. We've all been praying for you, but I'm so glad that you answered my letters. Maggie's talent is truly a wonder. If anyone can help you find some peace, she can. Have the police found anything?" she asked softly as she pulled away.

"They don't tell me anything." Laura shook her head. "I'm not family." She took a steady breath in through her nose to halt the threat of tears, a movement not unnoticed by her companions.

"Won't you sit down?" Maggie offered, surveying her with light green eyes. "You can tell me about her?"

As they took their seats at the round table, Laura could not fail to recognise that one of the chairs was dissimilar. While the others were comfortably upholstered, the one Maggie claimed was bare, uncushioned wood. Yet the most eye catching detail was the leather straps hanging limply from the arms.

"Laura?" Camila said, regaining her attention.

She shuffled in her seat, realising that she had been staring.

"Can you tell me about Katherine?" Maggie asked patiently.

Laura nodded, looking down at her hands. "Kathy, she was quiet. I could hardly get her out of the apartment to socialise, as if she would have had the time anyway. Kathy was a Macy's girl, worked the long hours. She was saving for school. Her parents- They didn't have any money, but Kathy was going to be somebody." Laura drew in a sharp breath as her hand clamped over her mouth. Camila came to her side at once and rubbed her back comfortingly.

A swell of pity twisted in Maggie's chest. Some of her sittings were different than others. Sometimes the loss was an aged, familiar burden, but with others, the grief was still palpable in the air. She should have known that today's appointment would be one of the latter. Maggie remembered reading about Katherine Read's death in the paper some weeks ago, so unexpected... and violent.

Laura pulled herself upright and wiped her eyes. "I'm sorry. It's just- I'm probably going to be a shopgirl forever, and that's alright. But Kathy, she really was going places. I just don't understand who would do this to her."

Neither did the police, if the papers were to be believed.

"I understand," Maggie consoled.

"I'm glad you came today, Laura," Camila said, returning to her seat and offering her an encouraging smile.

"Are there any questions you wish to ask her?"

Laura shook her head. "I suppose I just want to know if she feels peace now, if she's happy. And I want to tell her that- that I'm sorry." She brought her handkerchief to her eyes again.

Maggie allowed her a moment to collect herself. Once, she would have employed the restraints on her chair, an effort to prevent her from collapsing once she connected with a spirit. But over these past months, her ability to anchor herself to those at her table had grown, and the physical toll on her own person so lessened. For a time, Maggie employed them as a comforting measure, but she had forgone them some weeks ago when they proved wholly unnecessary.

"Shall we join hands?" Maggie said as Camila found her seat.

Camila reached for her at once, her confidence encouraging Laura to do the same. With their hands in her own, Maggie could feel their warmth pulsing against her skin. She closed her eyes, reaching out her senses beyond the boundary of the seen and to the icy whispers of the Nether.

"Call for her, Ms. Bennett," Maggie instructed, not opening her eyes.

"Kathy," Laura said, voice trembling slightly. "Can she hear me?"

Maggie sifted through the fog of a thousand voices, but none rose willingly to meet her.

"Try again," Camila encouraged.

"Kathy, it's me, Laura. Are you with us?"

A presence perked, drawing nearer. Maggie's hands tightened their grip as she focused on it, clearing the others away.

"I've found her," Maggie said. "Keep talking."

"Katherine," Camila said, "We want to speak with you."

"Kathy, can you hear us?"

Her name, spoken by a familiar voice, drew Kathy's consciousness from the depths of the void. As Maggie drew nearer, the chill of her presence wisped against Maggie's skin. Yet, she kept her mind on the warmth of her own body, on Laura and Camila beside her as she reached out to form the bond.

As the connection took hold, the parlor melted away. In Maggie's mind, a new image took shape as if from smoke until it took solid form around her. She was walking on a darkened, snowy street. Buildings grew from the shifting mist until they were towering over her. Other shadows moved around her, ill formed figures, passersby which Katherine had never committed to memory. Yet she could feel the snow seeping through her stockings as the wintry wind tugged at her coat, stinging her cheeks. Exhaustion weighed on her mind and body as she made her way home.

"She is with us," Maggie said as the memory played in her mind. "I see her walking home. It's very cold-" A gasp escaped her lips.

As Katherine's heart hammered in fear, so did her own. They were connected now, one and the same.

"What is it?" Laura asked worriedly.

"Maggie?" Camila tightened her hold on her hand.

A knife had been placed against her back, a firm hand on her shoulder. All sensations of the memory centered on the sharp point she could feel even through her coat. She tried to turn to see his face, but the knife only jabbed her more insistently. Under his grasp, she was steered off the sidewalk and into a narrow alleyway. Her feet stumbled as the sidewalk gave way to the uneven cobblestones.

"It's happening," Maggie said, unable to keep Katherine's fear from leaking into her own voice.

"Oh my God," Laura sobbed. Her hand slid from her own, and Maggie took in a sharp breath of frigid air.

"No, Laura, don't let her go," Camila urged.

Laura's hand held her tightly as, in the memory, Katherine's initial shock began to dissipate, giving way to true desperation. Already, she could no longer see the others who had been walking beside her only a moment ago. Their only company now was piles of snow and debris. Her lungs filled with air, preparing to scream. She should have done this before, the moment she felt the knife, but it wasn't too late. They could still hear her if she-

Something hard connected with her head, a fist, or even a rock. The pain swelled as the force of the blow sent her spinning. She caught herself against a cold brick wall.

"Maggie?" She heard Camila's distant voice as her head spun.

She had to stand, to run, but she could not find her bearings. The vision warped and blurred, the alley tilting beneath her feet. Only the support of the icy wall was keeping her upright. For the first time, she saw his face. Where she had expected to find a villain, a monster, she found only a stranger, a perfectly ordinary looking stranger. For a single second, a glimmer of hope rose inside her that the attacker had run away and this man was even here to help her. But then she saw the knife in his hand, and her hope turned to sickening dread. Why was he attacking her? The confusion and helplessness twisted inside her until she was shaking.

"I don't have any money," she said, if aloud or only in the memory, Maggie could not say. "Please-"

"Is she alright?" a faint voice asked.

Over her, the man's face remained unfazed. The knife raised ever so slightly. His hand was fidgeting with the handle, gripping it again and again as if to get it just right. Understanding washed over her, an icy wash of despair.

He was not here to rob her.

"Please," she begged, terror drumming in her heart as hot tears streaked her cheeks.

Maggie tried desperately to pull away. She had felt the blow to the head so clearly; all she could think of was that knife. But she had lost her way, too tangled in the memory to free herself, and Katherine would not let her go... Not until the man drove forward.

His body collided with hers, the knife impacting her stomach like a brutal fist. Yet as it withdrew, she could feel the blood pouring from her, the warmth spreading over her blouse. She was frozen, wrapped up in the pain, the surreal sensation of the hot blood spreading over her cold skin. Then he raised the knife again.

Maggie ripped herself from the memory. She surfaced in the parlor, skin pale and covered in sweat. The sound of Laura's sobbing filled her ears.

"Maggie?" Camila was standing before her. "Are you with us?"

She could barely decipher her question as the memory of the pain radiated from her stomach. Her heart was still racing, every nerve heightened. Maggie could still feel the blood pouring from the open wound, though her eyes told her that her shirt was stark and white. Her hands shook as she tried to reconcile with reality. It hadn't really happened. Well, it had, but it had happened to Katherine, not her. It had only been a memory.

"Maggie?" Camila's voice held the slightest hint of fear. It was an unnatural tone for her, enough to call Maggie from her thoughts.

"I'm sorry- I-" Maggie swallowed.

"Was she truly in so much pain?" Laura managed between her sobs, drawing both of their eyes. Camila put her arms around her in consolation. Her brown eyes flickered to Maggie over Laura's shoulder, the question in them clear.

Maggie nodded as she forced in another even breath. She made herself look down again at her clothes. There was no wound, no blood. The pain was only the echo of a memory, nothing more. Still, her hands shook. It was the oddest sensation to remember the phantom pain against her head, in her stomach. In the moment, in the memory, it had felt real. When she had returned to her own consciousness, it lingered. The pain, the fear, were unswayed by the wellness of her body or the familiarity of her surroundings.

"If you'll excuse me," Maggie said faintly, standing from her chair. Laura barely looked at her, too eclipsed by heartache to pay her any mind. "I am so sorry," she breathed before cutting to the door. Her footing was unsteady, but Maggie managed to make her way down the stairs numbly and into the apartment marked 320.

The sitting room was lit by a hearty fire. The heat of it was not enough to thaw the icy sheen of sweat which coated her skin. Maggie went to the cabinet bar and poured herself a generous cocktail with trembling hands. Once the glass was satisfactorily filled, Maggie sat on the settee beside the fire and took a long drink.

She should have known better, Maggie thought punishingly as she pressed her palm into her forehead. The ice in her glass rattled in her shaking grasp. After the events of only a few months past, with Charles, with Anne, she should have known better.

She was draining her glass when Camila came through the door to the apartment, closing it quietly behind her. Maggie watched her wordlessly, having no defense for herself. The shame was no doubt written clearly enough in her expression.

"Laura is on her way home," Camila said finally.

Maggie nodded, looking down at her glass and wishing there was more. It seemed to be the only cure for the lingering chill.

"Are you alright?" she asked, rounding the settee and sitting in the opposite armchair, Jonathan's customary seat.

"Me?" Maggie let out a brazen laugh. "What about her?" Camila looked down at her hands, so she pushed on. "She came to me for help, and-" Maggie shook her head. Laura had come to her for help, for solace, and what had she given her? Nothing but a window into Katherine's terror and pain.

Camila began slowly, deliberately. "I don't know much about these things, Maggie, but it seems to me that you can't control what the spirits show you."

That much was true, though it hardly felt like an excuse. She had the power to make a connection or to break one, a talent she had honed over these past months. But what they offered her, the ghosts, the echoes, was from their own will, never hers.

"I should have known better than to even try," Maggie said stubbornly.

"Why?"

She scoffed as if it should be obvious. "Her death, it was violent. It was horrible. The last time I encountered a spirit like that-" Camila nodded, sparing her from having to continue on. "There is no peace in waking them."

"You forget that I knew her too, and of course, it is horrible to think- to know that she suffered so terribly. But maybe it isn't peace that Katherine wants," Camila offered. "Maybe she just wanted to be seen."

Her words settled in Maggie's mind. Perhaps the worst part of Katherine's death was that she suffered it alone. No one had been there to share the burden of her suffering or even to bear witness, save her killer.

"Maybe," Maggie relented.

The weight of her admission hung over them for several moments before Camila shuffled, clearing the thickness from her throat.

"Have you heard from Charles lately?" she asked, trying to sound more casual in her inquiry, though it was clear she was not as unaffected as she appeared.

Maggie stood to pour another absolutely necessary drink. Charles had returned home to Virginia two months ago. Yet besides a brief, and maddeningly vague, letter to tell her that he had indeed arrived safely back at his childhood home, there had been nothing but silence. That is until two days ago.

"No," Maggie lied as the amber liquid sloshed satisfyingly into the crystal glass.

Camila nodded, seeing that this line of conversation would be a dead end and mercifully dropping it. Instead, as Maggie returned to the settee, Camila steered their talk to lighter topics. And as all roads lead to Rome, with the wedding just over two months away, it soon became their sole topic of conversation.

She was happy to oblige, nursing her drink as Camila complained about the stresses of planning the seemingly infinite details, going into animated retellings. Maggie was the perfect audience, offering condemnation and support when appropriate. Every so often, Camila would ask her opinion on this detail or that, which Maggie was happy to provide.

They were in a fit of laughter over something to do with the seating arrangements when Jonathan walked through the door, looking very busy. He glanced between them as he took off his rain soaked coat. Her brother was objectively handsome and kept his appearance tidy and polished. Though after a full day's work, Maggie detected faint wrinkles in his suit. A few of his sandy brown hairs had fallen out of place.

Camila stood to greet him as he set down his case. Jonathan was at least a foot taller than his slight fiancée, though he hardly seemed to care as he leaned down to kiss her on the cheek. Maggie had noticed that Camila had become accustomed to standing on her toes for such gestures. She wondered if she was even aware.

"Maggie, please tell me you are properly packed for tomorrow," Jonathan said. His tone was still set in his businesslike manner, as it often was when he'd just returned from the office.

"Tomorrow?" Maggie asked, arching a brow in a comically thoughtful expression. He'd spoken of nothing but their impending trip the whole week, and she was just tipsy enough to enjoy plucking at his nerves.

Her brother's face turned a slight shade redder. "Our engagement party," he bit out, "at Camila's parents' home in the country. Tell me you are packed."

"Oh, that. I'll pack first thing," she promised.

Jonathan let out an aggravated huff as he turned toward the study. He had converted the room into his office a year ago when she had claimed the upstairs parlor for her own purposes. It was a convenient solution as his bedroom lay just beyond, and Jonathan was fond of working late into the night.

"Where are you going?" Maggie asked.

"To pack, I-" he stopped red faced as Maggie let out a snort of laughter. Her brother turned on his heel. "You've had the whole day! I've been at work tying up loose ends. Not to mention, when I came in this morning, one of the office windows was broken. I spent the whole morning on inquiries that went nowhere-"

"She knows it's important, Jonathan. We all do," Camila said. "Go and pack."

She offered him a pacifying kiss that seemed to ease him slightly, enough to turn back on his way. Still, his footsteps were heavy against the wooden floor.

"You shouldn't pick on him so," Camila said pointedly. "He's got a lot on his mind now. You could do your bit to help things."

Maggie straightened herself on the settee and nodded, setting down her drink. "You're right. I'll be on best behavior this weekend, anything the both of you need."

Camila smiled. "I'll try not to take you up on that... too much."

CHAPTER
2

"YOU MUST STOP FUSSING, really," Maggie said.

Jonathan looked up from fidgeting with his watch chain to glance at her indignantly.

"Please, you're making me nervous." The car gave a creaking lurch, causing Maggie to drop her book to the floor. "How am I supposed to read while you're wound up tighter than a noose?"

"I just don't want to be late," he said, reaching down to retrieve the book. "Camila and her parents are expecting us and-"

"And we'll be there early because we left an hour before we had to." Maggie snatched the book from his outstretched arm. Camila had taken her car out to her parent's country home early that morning to help with preparations for the party, which would not start for a few hours yet.

"You know these country roads can be unpredictable," Jonathan argued.

"Speaking of-" Maggie began, interrupted by another bump in the road, causing her to scowl. "How much farther is this house of theirs? When Camila said outside the city, I didn't think we'd be travelling across the state."

Jonathan leaned forward, peering out the windows for all the good it would do. There were no real markers, nothing but endless fields and pastures outstretching to the horizon of rolling hills covered in evergreens. The sky beyond was bleak and grey. Even beneath her travelling coat, late winter's chill left her longing for the warmth of the fireplace back on Warren Street.

"It shouldn't be long now," Jonathan said, settling in again.

"You would think they would have a station closer to the house."

"Mr. Huddleston likes the quiet of the country. He has quite a bit of land out here as well. I wouldn't be surprised if we're passing through it now."

"I suppose the quiet is fine if you can overcome the smell," Maggie said, opening her book forcibly and beginning to read again.

Jonathan grimaced, and they returned to their silence. Nothing to her was duller than hours of travel, confined in a car or train, or worse, a cramped ship's cabin. In her younger days, Maggie had found it unbearable to be contained in such a manner for tedious, unending voyages to and from finishing school. She had learned to cope with the dull journeys by burying herself in books, poetry, and plays. Of course, her preference was for titles that would have never been allowed in her proper, well mannered school or household. In her final years at school, Maggie had even written her own works on occasion, mostly poetry, on topics that would have sent her parents and teachers into a fit.

Once, she had left such a piece in her desk by mistake. It seemed by the end of the day it had been passed through the entire student body, who discussed it in scandalous whispers until it was taken up by the staff. Days later, she even overheard two of her teachers discussing the creative and erotic nature of the work with esteem.

It was a relief when the large estate finally came into view. Well tended grounds surrounded the two story brick home. Its facade was decorated with many tall windows offering a narrow glimpse of the handsome furnishings within. Seeing the structure for herself, Maggie found it remarkably like Jonathan had described it to her, the molded arches above the door, the gardens overlooked by statuettes, all just as he said.

A footman was waiting at the end of the drive. He opened the car door and offered a hand as Maggie climbed out. Beneath her, her legs were stiff and sore as the blood began flowing through them once again. A pair of grooms were leading two carriage horses across the drive as Maggie followed Jonathan inside. They stopped obligingly to allow them to pass. The younger of the pair was rather dashing, in a rugged sort of way, Maggie thought as her eyes lingered on the finer points of his features. The horse he'd been leading tossed its head, nickering loudly. Maggie couldn't help it as she startled backward, clutching her chest. The towering beast shook its mane as Jonathan chuckled beside her.

"Oh, quiet," Maggie muttered as she marched ever more purposefully toward the stone steps.

The front doors were thrown open wide, inviting them in as if for a friendly embrace. Inside, the hall was filled with soft, pink peonies and cream roses collected in delicate porcelain vases. Their bold coloring and exotic design led Maggie to assume they were keepsakes from the Huddleston's time in India, where Camila had spent much of her childhood. Valets and maids circulated in and out of various doorways carrying food, decorations, and refreshments. Surveying the grandeur of the hall were the painted faces of many pristine works of art hung with care on the walls.

Camila stood in the middle of it all in a flowing dress of pink chiffon, which mirrored the same blush tone as the flowers around her. She oversaw the preparations, radiating with a nervous energy they could sense even from the entryway.

"You're here!" Camila exclaimed as she laid eyes on them, extending her arms to Jonathan as if embracing a savior. "Oh, thank Heavens. I could really use your help before the guests arrive."

"Camila, dear," called a woman's voice from another room.

The relief drained from Camila's spirit, returning to its frantic state.

"Coming, Mother," Camila said, hurrying into a large parlor where a long table was being adorned with tiered plates of treats, small cakes, and large bowls of refreshments.

Mrs. Huddleston, whom Maggie had never met but could not have been mistaken now in the flesh, was a small woman with the formidable presence only a mother could command. She supervised the work with the scrupulous eye of a general, examining every last detail. Her long black hair resembled Camila's in every way. In fact, she seemed responsible for many of Camila's finer features, though her complexion was much darker, the rich earthen shade of the subcontinent. Her gown even mirrored Camilas, though in a deeper rose shade.

In the corner, Maggie could see two young girls, who could only be Camila's sisters. The older looked no more than twelve, the younger only a few years behind. Each of them was dressed for the party. Their thick black hair was tied back with ribbons, but they had removed their gloves to snatch small sweets for themselves before ducking behind the tablecloth to consume them.

"Camila, is the entryway ready?" Mrs. Huddleston asked.

"Very nearly," Camila said. "Mother, this is Ms. Margaret Ward, Jonathan's sister."

"How very nice to meet you, Margaret. Camila has said so much about you." Her brown eyes were soft and sincere.

Maggie was just about to return a polite greeting when Camila's eyes widened. Two men had just entered the parlor carrying a large four tier cake between them.

"Mother," Camila said as if addressing the sudden appearance of a giant arachnid, "what flavor is that cake?"

"It's an angel sponge with strawberry and almonds, just like I ordered for-"

"Mother, no!" Camila gasped. "I told you I wanted a simple-"

"Well, I thought the occasion deserved something more." Mrs. Huddleston interrupted.

"Jonathan is allergic to nuts!" Camila exclaimed. "The cake could kill him, Mother!"

"No need to fret, dear. I will sort this out." Mrs. Huddleston said, leaving the room at a graceful and determined pace. She marched straight past her sticky fingered daughters, none the wiser, as they followed her out of the room politely with pockets full of goodies.

Camila sat heavily on a settee, and Jonathan took a place beside her.

"It will all work itself out," Jonathan soothed.

"This day has been such a disaster!" Camila began breathlessly, as if she had just run a great distance. "I arrived not an hour ago and at once had to address a circus with the flowers. And then my father brings up two cases of champagne and insists on having a toast! He ordered champagne, from France, for today after I expressly said I wanted it to be a sober event. What will the women from the movement say if they see me, after all my talk of temperance, toasting champagne!" Camila finished her speech on a nearly hysterical note.

"You just relax," Jonathan said, patting her hand thoughtfully. "Maggie and I are here to help. We will see that everything is just as it should be."

Camila seemed to stiffen her lip at his consolation, though such a vague promise would have never talked Maggie off such an emotional ledge.

Once she was more herself, Camila provided them both with a list of tasks to complete. The last fleeting hours before the guests arrived were spent running in every direction. They had been so busy it was a great relief when the first guests finally appeared. All that was left was to put on a gracious smile and well mannered composure to greet them.

More than a hundred persons must have passed through the door into the welcoming reception hosted by the Huddleston's manor. Maggie saw little of Camila or Jonathan as they were surrounded constantly by a crowd of wellwishers eager for their turn with the guests of honor. Instead, she contented herself to sample many of the treats from the open table, eavesdropping on others' conversations. She wandered the unfamiliar rooms, now and then catching a glimpse of Camila's mischievous sisters running through the halls, playing games and laughing gaily with the other children.

Maggie was taking a bite of a decadent lemon tart when she heard an altogether unexpected name enter the conversation of a pair of ladies only a few feet away. "...like Katherine Read..."

Her interest was piqued at once, and Maggie shuffled closer, keeping her eyes on the spread before her.

"It's almost enough to make one rethink returning to the city," one of them was saying, genuine concern coloring her voice.

"It's a terrible business," the other said, her tone hushed, "but it's not as if you work."

"Mary Foster didn't work," the first corrected. "I knew her, though rather distantly. Her poor fiancé will be heartbroken."

Maggie turned, putting on a friendly, concerned smile. "Terribly sorry to interrupt," she said, "but I seem to be behind on the news."

The young ladies looked about scandalously, seemingly able to forgive her forwardness for the opportunity to share what seemed a very excitable bit of gossip.

"It was in the papers yesterday," the second began. She had a round face and brilliantly red hair styled in tight curls. She dressed in a similar vermilion shade, setting her rather violently against the sea of pastels. "Mary Foster's death was connected with a murder from some time ago, Katherine Read."

"The police are saying it may be the same man," the first said.

The red haired one nodded, pursing her lips. "The papers are warning women not to travel alone or at night. They believe he may kill again."

All at once, the memory of Katherine's terror came over her, the chill of that alleyway, the pain as the knife plunged into her stomach. A wave of nausea coated her throat as a cool sweat coated her skin.

"Are you alright?" One of them was asking.

Maggie caught her breath and schooled her features. Just as she was about to offer a stream of well mannered excuses, she was spared.

Glasses began clinking all about them as Camila's father called for a toast. Maggie took a glass of champagne from a passing tray and turned her attention, thankful for the moment to collect herself. She could not process the significance of what she had just heard, not here. Today was for Jonathan and Camila, Maggie told herself as she pushed the storm of worries from her mind.

"Ladies, gentlemen, friends, family," Mr. Huddleston began in a deep voice. Camila's father was tall and appeared in remarkable strength for a man his of age. Despite his dark hair streaked with grey and his blue eyes creased by time, he was still very handsome. "Thank you for joining me today to eat my food and drink my champagne." A light laugh rolled through the crowd.

"In all seriousness, I thank you for coming to celebrate the engagement of our daughter to Mr. Jonathan Ward." The crowd applauded politely and glanced at Jonathan and Camila, who smiled as one does when on display. "I believe that the heart knows what it wants, who it wants, for those who are willing to listen. When I was stationed in India in my youth, I was not expecting anything more than to further my military career, to follow in the family tradition. I was too young then to know what it was I wanted for myself. That is until I met a lovely young woman."

He tilted his glass towards Mrs. Huddleston, who blushed warmly. "My heart spoke the moment I saw her, and I will be forever grateful that I listened. Of course, we endured our share of hardships. The divides of society marking us as separate in status, culture, and loyalty. Yet, we remained loyal to one another, and that bond has the strength to bend even the most rigid of obstacles.

"I share all of this to offer you one last piece of fatherly advice. Through whatever may come, remain loyal to each other, fight together even when life tries to form a division between you." Mr. Huddleston raised his glass. "Jonathan, my dear Camila, I wish you both many happy years as I have shared with my darling wife. Cheers."

Maggie raised her glass and took a drink. Her eyes flicked to Camila as she reluctantly took a minuscule sip of her own. Around her, the crowd went back to its congratulatory murmuring. Camila whispered something to Jonathan, and he kissed her cheek sweetly as they parted ways. Maggie smiled at her as she cut through the crowd toward them. Today was for her, Maggie reminded herself. She could concern herself with the probability of a ripper stalking the streets of her beloved city later.

"Camila," the two ladies greeted her with matching smiles.

"Sarah, Lily, I see you've met Margaret Ward," Camila introduced them politely. "Soon to be my dear sister-in-law."

They turned, assessing her with renewed interest.

"It was a pleasure," Sarah said.

"Will you be attending the rally in two weeks?" red haired Lily asked.

Camila nodded conspiratorially. "I couldn't miss it. As I've been saying for some time, New York is perfectly poised to make the decision. With the success that our cause has already had in the West, New York could be the beginning of true suffrage in the East. If we continue our campaigning, we may be able to push them to a vote by the year's end!"

"Do you really think?" Sarah said, eyes going wide.

"If my sources are to be believed," Camila said, flashing an enigmatic smile before turning her attention to Maggie. "You'll have to join us, Maggie. We will be campaigning just outside city hall."

"Well, that does sound marvellous," Maggie agreed with a coy smile.

CHAPTER 3

AFTER SPENDING TWO DAYS ENJOYING the hospitality of Camila's parents, relief washed over Maggie as their car made the final turn down Warren Street. Not that it had been an unpleasant visit. They were truly lovely people and gracious hosts. Though spending the entire weekend sandwiched between Camila and Jonathan, fearful that if her brother smiled much longer, he might indeed injure himself, was not her ideal. It was far too reminiscent of the days after finishing school when she had been living with her parents, smiling at one person after another, back rigid under her mother's constant vigilance. It had been clear that, in her parent's eyes, finishing school had not taken its course with her and that Maggie was very far from *finished*.

Not to mention, Maggie's thoughts had been entirely preoccupied with the news she had heard at the party. Later that evening, she had managed to get her hands on a paper and had confirmed that Mary Foster was killed in an alley, a death eerily similar to Katherine Read's. The police seemed to concur and suspected the same killer was still at large... A notion that had not sat well in her mind, to say the least.

The hour was already rather late when they came through the door of the apartment, travel weary and sullen. Maggie had hardly said a word to her brother on the journey home, not that Jonathan had been one for conversation either. A person can only take so many niceties before longing for much needed solitude. Maggie raised her eyes in silent gratitude as she saw that Mrs. Doyle, the housekeeper, had already set the table for dinner.

They ate in thankful silence. After supper, Mrs. Doyle cleared the table. Ordinarily, they would settle into seats by the fire, Maggie with a book and Jonathan with his pipe and paper, but tonight, even that was beyond her.

Maggie was just opening her mouth to excuse herself early to bed when Jonathan spoke first.

"A letter for you, Maggie," he said, holding out a letter from the stack of mail that had piled up during their absence.

A bit of energy sparked into her as she thought perhaps it was a letter from a prospective client or even her associate, Mr. Walter Davies. The postman had long known to deliver all postage addressed to her parlor directly to the apartment. A forbidden hope even flickered within her that it was a correspondence from Charles, but that was immediately, mercifully, squashed.

Most unfortunately, it was neither. The letter in Maggie's hands was addressed in her mother's sinister penmanship. A groan escaped her as Maggie slouched down into the settee to read it begrudgingly.

Dear Margaret,

I hope this letter finds you and your brother in good health. Your father and I very much regret being unable to attend Jonathan's engagement celebration...

Her eyes continued to scan the letter, only to widen in horror. She sat straight, her fingers tightening around the paper until she was strangling the offending page.

"Did you know about this?" Maggie demanded, shooting to her feet and shaking the letter furiously.

Jonathan looked up from the bundle of envelopes, pipe slack in his mouth.

"Know about what?" he asked, composing himself.

"Mother says that once you and Camila are married, I'm to move back home!"

"What?" Jonathan said, taking the pipe from his mouth and standing with her.

"She says I shouldn't intrude on you and her in the apartment and that it's time I move home."

Maggie's anger was fading into hopeless frustration, which always brought unwelcome tears to her eyes. Jonathan read the letter thoroughly as Maggie paced, fingers twisting themselves into anxious knots.

"Well," Jonathan sighed, "you wouldn't have to move back if-"

"Don't say it!" Maggie said, her voice becoming dangerously shrill. "I won't be forced! I won't!"

"It wouldn't be the worst thing if-"

"Jonathan, no! Not like this, not now! She can't do this to me!" Maggie sat heavily on the settee, her hands squeezing against her head as if she could crush it like a grape.

Jonathan paced back and forth before the fireplace, continuing to read the wretched thing in detail. "I don't suppose you got to the second page."

Maggie looked up with a dread filled expression. "It can't possibly be worse," she said, knowing full well that it certainly could.

Jonathan read aloud, "*We understand that with two months before the wedding, there is little time to find yourself a suitable match. As such, your father has arranged for the nephew of Mr. Cromwell from his alma mater, Mr. George Cromwell, to meet with you on Saturday, April the 14th, at 7 o'clock.*"

Maggie stood and snatched the paper, scanning the pretty cursive script until she found the lines in question. "They're sending another one? But that's the day of Camila's rally. I-"

"Well, maybe-"

"No, Jonathan, just don't," Maggie said, shaking in outrage. "He's going to be as self righteous, pigheaded, and dull as every other one they've sent."

"One day, you're going to have to pick one, you know."

"I don't *have* to do anything!" she growled.

"Well, you're never going to meet anyone suitable if you've already decided that they are all like you said," Jonathan said, hands perching on his hips.

"What if I just want to have my own life? I don't want to disappear into someone else's!"

"And what? Be a burden to me or Father for the rest of your life? Die an old maid?"

"Is that what I am to you? A burden!" Maggie shouted.

"You can't very well support yourself. Not with that hobby of yours," he argued in what she was sure he considered a practical tone.

"Oh, I'm such a hardship to you!" she retorted. "Let's not forget the checks Father sends you every month!"

"Maggie, please. That is not what I meant," Jonathan said, rubbing his brow with exasperation.

Maggie let out a rough breath. "I will meet him and eat with him, but I will not, as you and Mother would so enjoy, fall into some fairy tale foolishness," Maggie stated. "When it's over, you'll see. They are all the same."

With that, Maggie stormed back to her bedroom in a highly unladylike fashion and slammed the door violently behind her. On the other side, she realised she was still gripping the horrid papers. Letting out what was a debatable mix between a sob and a feral growl, she tore the pages in half and tossed the pieces to the ground. They fluttered to the floor as Maggie stood, hardening herself so as not to dissolve into some pitiful episode of tears.

After collecting herself for several moments, Maggie turned to her vanity, resigning to do something that was arguably far worse. Before she could stop herself, Maggie opened the drawer and pulled out the two letters written on the same thick parchment inked in the same short, even hand.

Charles had written the first correspondence only a week after they had last seen one another. He wrote about his safe arrival, how good it was to be home where he held such happy memories. Then his words flowed into another apology. *Though I know that I have made the right choice, my thoughts are with you often.*

When she had written back, her words had been cautious, polite. *I'm glad your journey was safe and comfortable... I too often hope that you are well.*

It had been weeks of silence before the second was delivered. She hadn't summoned the courage to look at the words again since it had first arrived, not until tonight. Maggie took it up with trembling fingers and opened it once more.

Dear Maggie,

I can find no other way to begin, but to offer my greatest regrets that I have not written to you sooner. These past weeks have been everything I had hoped for: a chance to see my family, to consider my future, and utmost to reflect on the events of the past, to heal. It was my hope that my next words would be of good news, heralding my return to New York, to you. Yet the unfortunate hand of circumstance has seen fit that I should be forced into doing the very opposite. I find myself in the agonising position of extending the distance between us for a second time.

My brother, Malcolm, has enlisted in the war in Europe. His announcement, only two years after the loss of our father, has broken my mother's yet fragile heart. As a son, as an elder brother, I could offer her but one consolation: that I would go with him to France and do everything in my power to see him home safely again.

It does not weigh lightly on my conscience, nor my heart, what this means for us, for what we may have become to one another. Nevertheless, I shall carry on in the hope that perhaps fate will be kind and there will be another chance for us. However, I cannot expect you to wait for such a day, nor would it be right that I ask it. I only ask that if I should return, I would have the chance to see you again.

And in the misfortunate case that such a day does not come, know that not only do I consider myself gratefully in your debt, but I hold you in nothing, if not the highest fondness and respect.

Yours, Charles

Maggie took in a stiff breath, but it was not enough to stop her from unraveling into shuddering sobs. The night it had arrived, she had cried until she was sure there couldn't have possibly been any more tears to shed on the subject. On that matter, Maggie found herself painfully wrong.

Jonathan blew out a breath of smoke irritably, eyes fixed on the settee opposite where his sister was hidden behind the day's paper. Being a man of routine, his mornings were predictable affairs: up early and dressed, a breakfast tray with tea, and then a read of the day's paper with his pipe by the fire. Yet the lattermost portion of his ritual had been hoodwinked before he had even finished his breakfast.

He cleared his throat loudly.

Maggie lowered the paper slowly, still reading whatever it was that had captured her attention so. After her outburst the night before, he had expected her to be somewhat sullen this morning, or even wrathful. What he had not been prepared for was whatever sort of peculiarity this was. Her brown hair was pinned haphazardly. Judging from the bags beneath her eyes, it seemed to him that she had been awake for some time, which was, in a word, odd. His sister had hardly ever been one for mornings. On many occasions when he left for the office, his sister had yet to even emerge from her rooms.

"Might I have a chance?" Jonathan said at last.

Maggie tore her eyes away.

"The paper?" he prompted, his impatience evident in his voice.

"Oh, yes." She pulled several sheets from the bundle and handed him the rest in something of a jumble.

"Thank you," he managed with a scowl that went unnoticed as Maggie rounded the settee to the door, heading up to her parlor, no doubt. He gave the paper a single shake, setting in to read, only to close it again after a moment and rub his brow tiredly.

Some hours later, Maggie was still in her parlor. The round table was almost hidden beneath newspaper cuttings. The discarded remains of the papers were scattered carelessly across the floor wherever they happened to fall.

Walter stood in the doorway to the parlor for several moments, watching as she rearranged the articles on the table, occasionally muttering to herself. Clearly, she had forgotten about their appointment, though it was equally obvious there was something else pressing on her mind.

At last, Walter adjusted his glasses and knocked softly on the open door. Maggie spun, surprised at his seemingly sudden appearance. Though as she took him in, brown suit and wire glasses, the doctor's bag faithfully at his side, the memory of their weekly appointment returned to her.

"Oh, Walter, I am so sorry. Please excuse this mess," she said, filled with nervous energy.

"It would seem to be the byproduct of an active mind." His round face offered her a brief, forgiving smile as he stepped inside. As there was no possible way of crossing the room without stepping on the scattered papers, he did not bother avoiding them.

"Yes, well, I would say so," Maggie said. "Goodness, what time is it?"

"Just after noon," Mrs. Doyle said pointedly from the doorway, carrying the tea tray. The housekeeper's brows were raised high in judgement beneath her red hair.

Maggie snatched several papers out of the way as she set the tray on the table.

"I'll not be cleaning this mess," Mrs. Doyle said as she retreated. "I am the housekeeper, not your nanny."

Walter cleared his throat as she disappeared around the corner, her footsteps carrying down the stairs.

"Tea?" Maggie said rather breathlessly.

"Yes, thank you," he said, brushing a few castoff papers aside so that he might take a seat.

As she prepared the tea, Walter glanced over the articles. Many from the last week but others as old as a month past, from mid February. All of which concerned a similar topic: the murders of those two women. He recalled reading that the police believed them to be connected, though he could admit that he had not been following the story.

"A terrible business," Walter commented as Maggie handed him his cup.

She looked at him perplexed for a moment, her tired mind thinking he was making some manner of comment on her offering.

"The papers," Walter clarified.

Maggie nodded, sitting down slowly.

"Can I inquire about your interest in them?"

"I had Ms. Laura Bennett in for a sitting last week," Maggie began. "She was Katherine Read's roommate and dear friend."

"I see," Walter said, his interest piqued.

"I made contact with Ms. Read's spirit, though I can honestly say it offered no comfort to anyone," Maggie said with a bitter laugh.

"Was it anything... Would it relate to your experiences with the late Mrs. Blackbourne?" he asked carefully.

"No," she answered tartly. "It was distressing in its own morbidly unique way." Maggie took a drink of the tea, letting the warmth spread through her chest. Anything to chase away the memory of that terrible alley. When she looked up, Walter was waiting for her to continue.

Maggie sighed, setting down her cup. "With Anne, I- I saw her die. I felt her fall, and then nothing... But with Katherine." She looked down to where her hands were gripping one another in her lap. She released them, flexing her fingers. "I saw her death. She wanted me to see, but... The first blow... It didn't kill her. She was so afraid. She knew what was coming... I had to let her go in the end. I had to break the connection. The pain- It was too much."

"My God, Maggie," Walter said, his eyes wide behind his wire spectacles.

"Which is why-" Maggie raised her voice slightly, reclaiming herself. "-if that man is still out there, I am determined to find him before..."

"You think you can find the killer?" Walter asked.

Immediately, Maggie began to shuffle through the papers until she produced a pencil sketch that had been hidden near the bottom.

"It shouldn't be too difficult," Maggie said as she slid the paper toward Walter. "Katherine saw him."

Maggie had done her best to craft his likeness in the early hours of that morning and was pleased with the result. His long face ended with a squared jaw. He might have even been handsome if it hadn't been for his overly large nose or ears that stuck out a touch too far. In the drawing, his hair was neatly oiled back, his round eyes set rather benignly beneath heavy brows.

Yet in Katherine's memory, Maggie recalled several locks coming loose during the attack. His eyes had been wide and manic, making him seem more disheveled, more monstrous than he appeared on the page. However, it would hardly have done to send out a search for a madman. When Katherine first saw him, her killer had seemed like an ordinary man, one she might pass on the street any day and never think twice.

Walter studied the image, a finger pressed to his lips before he spoke. "Hardly a remarkable appearance. Ambiguity might complicate matters."

"But it is a place to start."

He nodded. "Yes, and once we gather more evidence, this will certainly narrow our pool of suspects."

"You'll help me then?" Maggie asked, brows arched. "I know it is slightly outside our usual purview."

Walter nodded, setting the sketch down on the center of the table. "I'm not sure how much use I will be, but I will lend my talents as I can. This is an extraordinary circumstance, after all." He removed his glasses, cleaning them thoughtfully with a cloth as his eyes scanned the scattered articles surrounding the sketch. "It is a strange circumstance indeed when the living are more monstrous than the dead."

CHAPTER 4

THE MORNING OF THE RALLY was rather bleak, the sky overcast and generally gloomy. Dark clouds loomed with the real possibility of a hearty April shower. Of course, this was not ideal, but far too much preparation had gone into this event to balk at a drizzle. The movement's sources in the city government had been informed that there would be a significant vote concerning suffrage in the coming days. Camila was determined that her opinion on the matter be heard. Loudly.

Camila was running through a last minute list of preparations, primarily to ease her nerves as she stepped purposefully down Warren Street to fetch Maggie. The moment Camila crossed over the threshold of the apartment, it was clear that Jonathan and Maggie had been in the midst of an argument. During her time amongst the Ward siblings, Camila had learned that the two seemed to squabble almost endlessly, a byproduct of their vastly differing natures. These were, however, not arguments. The differences were subtle, but exceedingly important. First, in a proper argument, Jonathan's lips set in a particular way, creased and tense, and his hands would often find purchase on his hips. More noticeably, Maggie lost her flippant air and coy commentary and instead took on the persona of an irritable bull or some such stubborn creature.

Camila rarely interceded in squabbling, but as she entered the apartment to find her dear fiancé red faced with fists clenched at his sides and Maggie fuming as if about to charge, she could not help but put herself between them.

"Maggie, I do hope you're ready," she said amicably.

"I would be if it hadn't been-" Maggie growled.

"Why don't you finish up then?" Camila interrupted decisively.

Maggie took a deep breath, glowering at her brother once more, before exiting back to her rooms to make the final adjustments to her appearance.

"What on earth are you two on about now?" Camila asked once she was out of earshot.

Jonathan sighed, hands settling on his hips. "Our parents have set an appointment for her with a gentleman this evening. She's rather tense about the subject."

"And?" Camila probed.

"And I suggested that attending this morning's rally might not be the most prudent course," he admitted.

"You should know better than to stand in her way by now." She shot him a coy smile.

Jonathan cracked a begrudging smirk. "Shouldn't I?"

Maggie emerged into the sitting room, still fastening the last pin in her hair. Her gaze flashed from Camila to her brother, who seemed to be sharing some sort of joke, which she chose to ignore as she found her coat.

"We'll be back this afternoon," Camila said as she followed Maggie toward the door.

Jonathan leaned down and kissed her on the cheek.

"You will be careful, won't you?" Jonathan said nervously.

"Of course we will," Camila deflected. "There will be two dozen of us, or more, and we'll be right on the steps of city hall."

Jonathan waved them off, albeit tensely, and Camila followed Maggie out to the street.

Maggie glanced up at the ominous clouds with a scowl, hoping they wouldn't get caught in more than a sprinkle. Getting through the day dry seemed too farfetched to hope for. Nonetheless, they hailed a cab and directed it to city hall. Camila talked the whole way about who would be in attendance, the implications of their success. Maggie followed as well as she could, but was admittedly far less knowledgeable about such politics.

As Maggie stepped out onto the sidewalk, she could already hear the calls from the steps of city hall. A wave of excitement washed over her as Camila came to her side. Arm in arm, they rushed to join the others.

There was a great diversity gathered, old women beside young. A few had even brought little ones wrapped snugly in their carriages or held on hips. Some were dressed in the latest fashions. Others were of more meager means, but it hardly mattered. They were united under the colors of the movement, purple, white, and gold, worn on sashes or buttons over their long woolen coats. Others carried signs painted with messages such as "Equal rights for all!" and "Don't deny us our democratic liberties!". Lest their purpose escape anyone's attention, a large banner was planted beside them emblazoned with VOTES FOR WOMEN in bold, unyielding letterhead.

"It's already taken hold in the West!" a woman shouted down to those who passed below. "We can bring suffrage to the East! Votes for women!" The speaker set her sights on a man passing on the street. "Sir! Your daughters deserve the right to control their destinies!"

The man stopped and regarded her with a polite nod before continuing on his way.

"Votes for women!" Camila called as they joined the others.

The speaker turned to her with a wide smile. "Camila!" she greeted, her voice somewhat hoarse.

They shared a brief hug before she looked to Maggie. She was older than they were by a number of years. Friendly laugh lines marked her eyes. A touch of grey was coming to her hair, but she had a vibrant, youthful energy about her even so. "You must be Margaret."

"Maggie, please."

The speaker nodded. "I believe Amelia has some spare sashes."

"Amelia Simpson?" Camila asked, an air of surprise in her tone.

The older woman sighed, pointing them to the other side of the crowd.

Maggie followed their gaze to a dark haired woman holding a sign taller than she was. From the cut of her fur trimmed coat and delicate hat, it was clear that she came from no small amount of family money.

Camila thanked the speaker, who then resumed her post.

"You know her?" Maggie asked as they made their way toward Amelia.

"We've met on spare occasion. Her poor brother, Russell-" Camila shook her head. Maggie's mind worked, realisation dawning on her the moment before Camila explained. "He was engaged to Mary Foster, the woman who..."

"Yes," Maggie said sparingly.

"We should offer our condolences."

Maggie nodded in agreement as they approached her.

"Amelia," Camila greeted her, a touch of sympathy in her tone. "It is good to see you here. Mrs. Lewis told us you might have some extra sashes."

Amelia nodded toward a picnic basket at their feet.

As she was closest, Maggie retrieved one for each of them.

"We were both so sorry to hear about Mary," Camila said as Maggie stood once more. "It was so unfortunate that I missed the funeral. I never got to offer my condolences. How is your brother coping?"

Amelia's jaw tensed. "Not well. In all honesty, I never loved Mary much. And I don't mean to say that she wasn't a nice or good person. We just never got on. Maybe it was that she was too nice. But my brother really did love her."

"Of course." Camila nodded.

She shook her head bitterly. "When he proposed, you know how much he spent on that ring? He could have used our grandmother's, but he said she deserved nothing less than a diamond. It cost him a fortune."

"I'm sure it meant a lot to her," Camila reasoned.

From the look on Amelia's face, the intensity growing in her voice, Maggie sensed Camila was missing her true point.

"Did you know that the man who killed her didn't even take it?" she said, as if the fact disgusted her. "He could have walked away with a fortune in his pocket, and he didn't even bother."

"Well, at least-" Camila began, taken aback, but Amelia's eyes flashed with anger.

"Don't you understand what that means?" she snapped. "He didn't kill her for money. And there's no way in hell that *Mary Foster* ever made someone angry enough to *murder* her. That bastard killed her just to watch her die."

Maggie's skin chilled as Camila fell silent, jaw slack and a horrified look in her eyes.

"We understand," Maggie ventured, keeping any measure of pity or shock from her voice. It was clear that Amelia was after neither.

"Do you?" Amelia stepped closer, her voice lowering to a growl. "She meant absolutely nothing to that man. Until we have equality, that's all any of us will be, their playthings." She turned her attention out toward the passersby in the park. "I know it would look better if I stayed home and cried over poor Mary. You're probably not the only ones who judge me for coming out to something like this so soon. God knows my mother doesn't understand it. But I suppose this is how I grieve. I'd rather stand and fight, maybe even change things...."

Silence hung over them, even amidst the shouting crowd about them.

"You're right," Camila said firmly, putting on her sash. "We need to win this, for Mary. We won't give up."

And neither will I, Maggie agreed silently as she slipped the sash over her head.

Amelia regarded them for a moment before turning back to her post.

Maggie followed Camila as she found them a place among the others, and then it began. The speakers rotated to spare the voices. They called endlessly, sometimes picking out passersby, especially those on their way into city hall. More than once, a woman heard their calls and joined their number. More than once, someone had called for them to go home, be silent, mind their place, or some such unsavory sentiment, men and women alike. It was the latter that confounded Maggie. She could not understand why any woman of sound mind would want to limit herself. The speaker, whoever it was, never engaged with the naysayers, and that was eventually ample medicine to see them soon disperse, even if Maggie would have preferred to wring some of their necks instead.

It was more than two hours, and one small spot of rain later, that the doors of city halls opened wide, dispensing a crowd of men in nearly identical suits. The attention of all the ladies gathered turned toward them, the speaker calling enthusiastically for any of them to offer news of the impending vote. Maggie called along with them for answers. Her frustration mounted as each of the men ignored them forcefully, even as they passed only feet away on the steps.

"We deserve a government that represents the needs of women!" the woman to Maggie's left called. She stood only a few steps below, offering up a flower tied with a purple ribbon to them as they passed. Maggie watched as one of them, an older man, shoved her out of his path.

She tumbled down a few steps as the surrounding women gasped and tried to break her fall.

Fury heated Maggie's cheeks as she charged forward. "Don't you touch her!"

The man barely glanced at her, huffing at her audacity before moving on with an indignant stride down the steps.

Maggie's chest heaved with anger as she watched him go. Behind her, she could hear Camila asking the woman if she was alright. She turned to see her on her feet. A few locks of her curly hair had fallen loose over her freckled cheeks. Her clothes were plain, likely home sewn.

"Only bruised," she sighed.

Camila nodded sympathetically and offered encouragement as Maggie set out her gaze to find the man responsible. From Main Street around the corner, Maggie caught sight of his balding head as he spoke with a policeman. She watched as he indicated clearly in their direction.

Maggie elbowed Camila purposefully, directing her attention as a second officer joined the first. She only gave a slight nod, confirming that she understood. They wove through the crowd to the speaker, with whom Camila shared the news in hushed tones. The woman nodded, and Camila took her place, raising her voice. "As all men are created equal, women are not their subservients. All are equal in the sight of God as it should be in the law!"

As the officers came to the steps, Maggie squared her shoulders. If the others were standing their ground, she would not back down.

"Alright!" the younger of the two officers boomed. "You've said your piece. It's time to go on home now."

"We have the right to assemble!" Camila shouted for the benefit of the passerby. "Our constitution-"

"This disturbance must disperse-"

"Votes for women!" someone in the crowd bellowed, perhaps Amelia.

The policeman's face was naturally ruddy but reddened further into a deep, violent shade. "That's enough," he said, grabbing Camila by the wrist.

Camila let out a little shriek of surprise as Maggie pushed herself between them. "Let go of her," she demanded.

Behind her, a child started to cry.

He rounded on Maggie angrily just as the older officer put his hand on his shoulder, giving him a stern look. After a moment, he unhanded Camila, who eyed him venomously.

"Ladies," the older voiced loudly. His tone conveyed only passive annoyance at the situation. "You can disperse now, or we can take you in, and yer husbands can come deal with ya. Choice is yours."

CHAPTER
5

MAGGIE AND CAMILA STOOD ARM TO ARM, leaning against the metal bars of the holding cell. Beyond were a dozen or so desks, most of which were empty. The others were manned by officers who glanced back occasionally to see if they had broken. It was as if admitting how tired they all were or complaining about the wretched smell, the rude remarks from their drunken neighbors in the next cell, or the three hours they had been made to wait without contacting their families would be allowing the enemy to win.

At home, Jonathan was likely tying himself in a knot over why they had not returned. The possibility of making it to her dinner with George was becoming more remote by the minute. Of course, an evening in this dismal cell would be arguably preferable if it would not put her in even hotter water where her parents were concerned. The situation was not one she wished to aggravate, nor was her poor brother's nerves. Though she did not want to be the one who broke the silent vigil of her fellow ladies, Maggie had also had quite enough of being stuffed in the cramped cell like a sardine in a can.

The solution she came to was neither dignified nor altogether mature, but desperate times... Maggie waited for a particular officer. He was younger than most of the others, with soft, boyish features. When he gazed back at them, there was sympathy in his eyes. Finally, he stood, his attention preoccupied with whatever had called him from his desk. Once he was close enough, Maggie swooned, calling upon every bit of drama within herself as she collapsed to the ground amid a cloud of startled gasps.

Within seconds, a dozen hands were fanning her face as she lay there, limp as a fish. Outside, Maggie could hear the young officer undoing the lock.

"Step aside. Give her some air," he said chivalrously.

My hero, Maggie thought, schooling her brow into a pained crease.

"Maggie?" Camila asked anxiously.

Maggie opened her eyes blearily, taking in the many faces peering down at her.

"Are you alright, miss?" the officer asked.

"Yes," Maggie said faintly, resting a delicate hand on her brow for extra effect. "It must have been the heat. I'm so sorry. I have such a weak constitution.."

Camila helped her to her feet, and Maggie took an unsteady turn to reinforce her charade.

"Come with me," he said. "We'll get you some water."

Maggie looked back at the others as if conflicted before nodding. Following the officer out of the holding cell, she took in the first breath of fresh air she'd had in hours.

"Is there someone you can call to come and get you?" he said, offering her a chair beside his desk.

"My brother," Maggie said. "He'll be so worried about us."

"Of course, write the number here, and I will notify him."

Maggie smiled and nodded as she scribbled the number onto the paper. The young officer took it and promised to return with a glass of water. When he was gone, Maggie offered a brief nod to Camila, who returned it knowingly.

As she waited, Maggie's curious eyes wandered over the officer's desk, but all the papers were on disappointingly mundane matters. However, the desk just behind her was much busier, thick folders piled upon one another at odd angles. Maggie glanced around the room, but none of the men were paying her any particular attention. When she was sure no one was looking, she casually flicked open one of the folders.

At once, a chill prickled over her skin. Her focus honed as she felt the beckoning call of a presence reaching out beyond the boundary of the void. Resting on the top of several files was a velvet choker. A single stone rested in the center. It was clearly a costume piece. The scarlet gem was scratched in many places, the velvet worn from use. Yet, Maggie could not take her eyes off it. A single whispering voice emerged from the mist so clear she could almost understand it... Almost. The police station faded from her mind as she reached for the necklace.

The stone against her skin was like ice. At once, Maggie plunged into the darkness as the presence gripped her. She gasped, but the frigid breath caught in her throat. Panic beat against her chest as she tried in vain to fill her lungs with air. She couldn't breathe. Distantly, Maggie knew she was falling, but her focus was shifting away from her own consciousness. A new reality was forming vaguely around her. Maggie clung to it in desperation.

Suddenly, she was grasping at threadbare sheets as she lay in a bed not her own. Strong hands were pushing down on her neck. She couldn't breathe. The stone of her necklace was cutting into her throat.

No, this wasn't her, Maggie told herself, but reason was nothing to her as she fought for air.

Her eyes darted around, looking for someone, anyone, to stop this. The room was covered in faded floral wallpaper, water stained and peeling in many places. Even the sheet beneath her was damp in the corner by her head. There was a door in the very corner of her vision, but it was shut and silent. It was hard to see much more as the hands around her neck held her firm. Her lips formed silent pleas as she stared at the door. No one came.

Her focus turned as her hands gripped the arms of her attacker, her fingers digging into his skin in desperation. Then she saw it, that face. His veins were strained on his temple, grey eyes wide and angry. Maggie's scream caught in her throat. She thrashed and clawed as darkness began to crowd her vision.

Then she felt it, beneath her hand, the beat of a living heart. Instinctively, Maggie pulled herself toward its warmth with all her will.

The material plane collided with her senses as Maggie gasped for precious air. She had fallen to the floor, a number of faces now distorted on the edges of her vision. Her body thrashed, pushing against the hands that held her shoulders against the floor. Her chest heaved greedily, only to exhale a desperate scream. It was as if every ounce of her fear was trying to leave her at once. No matter how loud she became, it was not enough.

"Be still!" A man's voice cut through her undiluted panic. "Yer safe, I'm not hurtin' you. Calm down!"

His voice drew her attention to his face. He was a stranger to her, not the killer. Beyond him, the police station… As reality settled over her, Maggie realised she was gripping his uniform so tightly her knuckles were white. As she loosened her grip, he did the same.

"There you go," he said, his lilting voice easing with relief.

His clear blue eyes studied her face from beneath his drawn brow. His jaw was rounded and clean shaven. A few long strands of reddish brown hair had fallen into his face. Maggie found herself locked in his gaze as she tried to steady her uneven breaths, focusing on the rhythm of his heart. It beat ardently, strong and defiant of the coldness beyond, anchoring her.

"It was him," Maggie said, unsure why.

The officer's eyes shifted from concern to guarded confusion.

"Maggie!" Jonathan said, claiming her attention as he pushed his way through the gathered crowd. "God, Maggie, are you alright?"

"Jonathan," Maggie said. The officer at her side moved to stand. For a moment, her hand gripped him tighter, and his blue eyes flicked to her in surprise. Maggie caught herself and let him go, shivering as his warmth left her. "When did you get here?" she asked.

Her brother's appearance was rather unkempt. To an ordinary person, it would have seemed like a rushed morning. Yet, Maggie knew him too well. To leave the house with his tie loosened, with his hair mussed on the side, he was in a state.

"In time to hear you screaming," Jonathan said, glaring at the officers watching their reunion and settling on the one who had been trying to calm her. "What on earth is going on here? I swear if any of you hurt her."

"I'll be fine," Maggie said, trying to ease the situation while battling the bouts of nausea threatening to up heave her at any moment. It wasn't any of their fault what had happened.

"What is your name, officer?" Jonathan demanded, ignoring her assurance.

"Officer Mulligan," he said almost defiantly. "Not a soul here laid a hand on her. She went into a fit. She needs a doctor."

Mulligan indeed, Maggie thought to herself, his Irish roots evident in the lilting manner of his voice.

"She collapsed earlier in the holding cell," said the young officer who had released her.

At last, Maggie managed a slow breath. Her brother's face was white as a sheet.

"I'll be callin' for an ambulance," Officer Mulligan said.

"I'm okay now, really," Maggie promised stiffly.

Jonathan hesitated, searching her with a knowing glance before nodding and helping her to her feet.

"That won't be necessary," Jonathan said. "I'll be taking her home, my fiancée as well." He nodded toward the holding cell where Camila was pressed against the bars, watching them.

Officer Mulligan's expression hardened, scrutinising her once more as Maggie did her best to feign wellness. After a moment, he nodded, though it was clear enough he did not believe her. Jonathan watched stone faced as they retrieved Camila. The two of them escorted Maggie to a chair to convalesce before they went to post the bail. She listened distantly as Camila tried to convince Jonathan to bail out the others as well.

Maggie could not follow their conversation any further. Her mind was still swimming in the horrors that she had seen. Her sights drifted back to the necklace. She shivered, still sensitive to its chill even from the other side of the room. Her gaze lifted and then froze. Officer Mulligan was seated at the desk where she had found the choker, watching her with a burrowing look. Genuine fear gripped her as to what he might find there.

"Maggie!" Her brother's sharp call drew her attention, and Maggie stood carefully to follow them.

The cab ride home was a silent affair. Jonathan was fuming, but Maggie was well submerged in her own thoughts. She was sure that the killer was the same man who had killed Katherine Read, but the woman through whose eyes she had seen was decidedly not Mary Foster. Mary had been stabbed in an alley, not strangled in a bedroom.

Maggie drifted through the front door of the apartment and sank into a seat on the settee. Only after a moment did she realise that Jonathan and Camila were speaking around her, arguing, in fact.

"-The whole ordeal was completely unlawful," Camila was saying.

Jonathan crossed his arms, his mind working furiously behind wide eyes. He took in a voluminous breath through his long nose. "It's alright," Jonathan said, looking to Camila. "I forgive you."

"I am forgiven?" Camila repeated in an indignant tone, the danger of which seemed to elude Jonathan as he carried on.

"Just promise me," he said, taking her hand, "that this will be the end of it."

"What?" she recoiled, snatching her hand away.

Jonathan looked up at her, alarmed at the reaction he had not foreseen. Maggie sank back into the settee, wishing to disappear from the scene she knew would play before her.

"Is that what you are hoping for?" Camila's voice was shrill, in a frightening way that neither Maggie nor Jonathan had ever experienced before. "A wife to just sit at home waiting for you with nothing of my own, no thoughts, no work, no rights! Just a mother and a maid for you!"

"What sort of mother goes about getting taken in by the police!" Jonathan demanded, finding his feet in the argument.

Camila looked back at him as if he had reached out his hand and struck her across the face.

"If that's the kind of woman you think I am, maybe we are both very wrong about each other," Camila said.

She was out the door before Maggie or Jonathan could process another thought. Maggie watched her go, feeling a great swell of pity for them both. That is until Jonathan opened his mouth.

"This is your doing," he accused her in a whisper.

"You blame me for this?" Maggie asked, aghast. "I haven't done anything!"

"You made her wild, like you. She was so sensible before you two started doing things together. You've corrupted her."

Maggie laughed humorlessly. "Maybe she is right. You don't know her at all."

Jonathan looked at her with more anger than she had ever seen in her brother's eyes, the kind only bred by deep, wrenching pain.

"Go and get dressed," he ground out.

"What?" Maggie asked, having no earthly idea what he was talking about.

"Your Mr. Cromwell will be here in a matter of an hour."

Dread poured over her like a bucket of ice. "Oh God, I can't, Jonathan, not today."

"You will, or Mother will have you shipping home on the next train. Though maybe that would be best," he uttered before storming off to his rooms.

Maggie stood in the sitting room utterly wounded, unsure how she would pull herself together for the wretched ordeal awaiting her.

CHAPTER

6

MRS. DOYLE FASTENED MAGGIE into her dress at a quarter to seven. She had picked out the first gown her fingers had found, one her father had brought back from Paris last Christmas, along with several others. The silk was deep blue, hidden beneath a layer of black beaded lace that made up the sleeves and decorated the collar. The beading covered the skirt, culminating in countless strands hanging from the hem to brush the floor. Maggie had fixed her curly hair in a dark bun, leaving a few pieces to fall into her face, a constant nuisance to her mother that she did now out of habit.

Maggie was still in front of her vanity when the doorbell rang. She listened to the muffled sound of his voice as Jonathan invited Mr. Cromwell in and told him that she would surely be out in a minute. Her exhausted expression looked back at her in the mirror. Maggie could nearly hear it begging her not to leave, to feign a head cold and crawl into bed. However tempting, such a decision would only make the matter worse. She stood with a deep breath and prepared to swallow the bitter pill before her.

In the front room, Jonathan stood by the fireplace talking to a clean cut man who must be the most recent delivery from her parents, George. He was tall, though not taller than Jonathan, with light hair and blue eyes. From his angular jawline to his full brows, he was undeniably attractive. His classically tailored suit and manner made it clear that his roots ran deep in wealthy soils.

As Maggie entered, Jonathan looked to her, but George did not turn, still deep in conversation.

"...but in this sort of economy, investment can only be encouraged. My father has been buying stock in a variety of industries here in America. He's always saying that industry is moving West, and so must the money. I can say that I, myself, do enjoy seeing the innovation of you Americans. You have such a thirst for everything modern. It's thrilling. Though, I must say I do prefer my home in Britain. When it comes to the arts, a country steeped in rich history and culture is simply superior in taste and refinement."

"Mr. Cromwell," Jonathan said, cutting in as he at last took a breath from his speech. "May I introduce my sister, Margaret." It seemed he had buried his previous anger under a thick layer of niceties. It reminded her far too much of their mother, who was capable of flipping her manner like the sides of a coin.

Maggie put a forced smile on her face, not pleased with being made to hover in the doorway before being properly introduced.

"I have been looking forward to our meeting since your father arranged it," George said in greeting.

"A pleasure," Maggie said reflexively, as he kissed her hand.

"I must say, I am unfamiliar with the area, having only been on this side of the pond on spare occasion." He flashed a smile she supposed was meant to charm her. "But I have chosen a restaurant which I believe will prove up to standard."

"I know of a place east of here--" Maggie began, but he continued to speak without interruption or hesitation.

"If you are ever in London, I must take you to this lovely dinner spot overlooking the Thames. They serve a lamb rare enough to melt in the mouth." He put on his hat as Mrs. Doyle helped her into her fur trimmed coat. "Mr. Ward, my good man, I shall have your lovely sister returned to you at a decent hour, shall I?"

Jonathan nodded and seemed about to speak, but George resumed his monologue as he offered his arm to Maggie and began to lead her out the door. She allowed herself to be swept away until the comfort of their apartment disappeared from view.

George's car was waiting for them outside. He helped her in with all the grace and manners of a gentleman. Her mind was fuzzy, consumed and confused by the constant cloud of chatter which George emitted into the air as if it were his life's breath. As the car rolled into motion, Maggie's better sense urged her to make some daring escape before they reached their full speed. However, social convention kept her firmly planted. There was no choice now but to resign herself to whatever the night would bring.

George supplied a steady stream of advice and anecdotes throughout the ride. Maggie's attempts to join in the would-be conversation had long ended by the time they reached the restaurant. The place was familiar to her. She had been there once or twice before. It was one of the most expensive spots in the city, though it had never been a favorite of hers. However, she was not given the time to mention any of this and didn't bother, given the slight chance that such a remark would be heard.

Maggie walked briskly out of the cold and into the warm atmosphere of the restaurant on George's arm. The interior was as opulent as their inflated prices might suggest, complete with plush seating and elegant table linens, sparkling chandeliers and fresh cut flowers. Many well dressed waiters bustled about with trays of food and dishes. Maggie recognised places like this when she saw them, where the rich came to spend outrageous sums simply to prove they could. Clearly, George was trying to impress her with his own fiscal flippancy.

"May I take your coat, sir?" the host asked in an austere manner, carefully honed to inflate the ego of their patrons to dangerous levels.

Wordlessly, George handed him his hat and helped her out of her coat, handing it to the man before removing his own.

"This way, sir, miss," another waiter said, coming alongside them.

Maggie placed her hand lightly on George's arm as they followed. Many of the tables were occupied, though the space hardly seemed full. The lights were dimmed and intimate. The air was filled with the buzz of many conversations and the smells of fine food and tobacco.

George pulled out her chair, and Maggie took her seat gracefully. A rather attractive young waiter came, presenting a bottle of wine that George sent back, requesting another. He boasted the quality and virtues of the vintage to her until it arrived, insisting it would be the best wine she had ever tasted.

"It was just the perfect year," he continued as the handsome waiter poured the vintage into her glass. "You know, the grapes were grown only miles from my family estate. When you visit, I will have to show you our countryside. It is idyllic in the spring. We have the most exquisite gardens, and there is nowhere better for riding than the moors. You do ride? They must have taught you in finishing school. Your parents informed me you were schooled outside of London."

"Yes, I was," Maggie managed.

"You'll find I have a passion for horses. I have had much success in breeding thoroughbreds since my boyhood. They are such magnificent beasts. Your father and I spoke of them for some time. He seemed quite impressed with the success of my star stallion, Excalibur Cross. I personally believe that he has the merit to race at the Cheltenham Festival. With all respect to your father, I find his claims that the American triple crown could ever rival the prestige of the English circuit preposterous. The thoroughbred, otherwise known as the *English* thoroughbred, can trace its roots back to British soil, as do most great things..."

Maggie had taken to consuming her wine at an accelerated pace, absently sipping between polite nods. As she finished her second glass of what she considered substandard pinot noir, she had nearly faded all of her conscious attention away from George's ramblings.

"...would you?" George said, pulling Maggie out of her thoughts and into the present reality.

"Excuse me?" Maggie asked innocently, having absolutely no idea where his monologue had carried him.

"Would you be agreeable?" he repeated.

"Oh, I believe so," Maggie said pleasantly.

"Very good," he said. "I think it's paramount in a marriage-" He stopped mid sentence as Maggie began to cough and sputter, choking on her drink. "Are you alright?"

"Please-" Maggie wheezed once she had regained her breath. "Please, excuse me. I will only be a moment."

Maggie stood from the table and made her way quickly to the powder room without looking back, very nearly tripping over an errant chair leg in the process.

Thankfully, the powder room was empty. Maggie sat down unceremoniously on the settee, her mind buzzing in agitation. She took deep, heavy breaths to calm herself until she caught sight of her reflection in the mirror. In the polished face staring back at her, Maggie saw a spirit tamed and broken. Its anger burned through her tears. The fury of a caged animal, of her forced hands, blazed a trail down her cheeks. The thought of becoming silenced, absorbed into the identity of another... Into a life like her mother's, a life of proper constraint... Trapped in some English country manor to what? Make children and keep a house?... No room for individuality or thought... or her.

Maggie grabbed the first thing she could reach from the side table and tossed it against the wall with all her strength, letting out an angry cry. The delicate vase shattered tremendously. A moment of savage satisfaction passed as her chest heaved, staring down at the ruined shards. The hot rush of anger washed away as the sounds of footsteps outside interrupted her solitude. Regaining herself, Maggie dried her eyes, trying desperately to regain her composure.

"Miss? Is everything alright? I heard a crash," a man's voice called through the door.

"Yes, I'm so sorry. I've just had an accident." Maggie called back more casually than she had thought herself capable.

The handsome waiter who had brought their wine entered hesitantly.

"So sorry to intrude," he apologised. "Are you alright, miss?"

"Yes, I am so sorry. I'm so clumsy."

"I will have it cleaned, miss. Is there anything else I can do for you?"

"No, thank you." Maggie turned from him and returned to the dining room.

George perked up at the sight of her and stood to offer Maggie her chair.

"Feeling better?" he asked, truly waiting for an answer for what seemed the first time all evening.

"Actually, I think I am feeling rather unwell," she answered honestly.

His brow furrowed thoughtfully. "You look feverish. I will have the check at once," he said, raising his hand for the waiter.

Minutes later, he was escorting her back out through the cold and into the car. He was going on about the weather and her health and something about his sister, but Maggie was paying little attention. Her head spun mildly from the drink. The rest of her was sick with regret for ever agreeing to leave the house at all.

"Perhaps we can see each other again when you are improved," George said as he walked up the steps to the Warren Street apartment.

"Yes, perhaps," Maggie agreed with a weak smile, eager to get inside and shell off this godforsaken dress.

"In any case, I wish you a speedy recovery." Maggie looked at him before going inside. To his credit, there was sincerity in his eyes.

"Good night, Margaret," George said before kissing her hand in farewell.

"Good night," she echoed before turning to the door and disappearing within.

She pulled off her coat and hung it tiredly. Her bed called to her with a siren's song, promising a quick and heavy sleep, and she was eager to answer it.

"Seems dinner went well," Jonathan commented from his seat by the fire.

Maggie only had the energy to glare in his direction.

Jonathan sighed and stood. "I'm sorry, Maggie, for what I said earlier. I don't think it would be best if you went back home. I understand how unhappy you were there."

Maggie straightened, unaccustomed to such frank acknowledgement of their parents' failings, at least not from him.

"I also see how unfair this all is, putting a clock on your engagement. It cannot be an easy expectation to live under."

"You'd be right in that assumption," Maggie agreed grimly.

"So I take it that George was not a winning suitor, then?"

"I will not be marrying *him*, if that's what you're asking."

Jonathan nodded. "I may be able to find some more suitable options at the club, if-"

Maggie shook her head. "No, please, the very last thing I want is-"

"I understand," he said, raising his hands. "Get some rest. You look wretched."

Maggie grimaced and turned toward her room, thinking only of the comforts of her feather coverlet and the sweet oblivion of sleep.

CHAPTER

7

MAGGIE ROSE LATE and set her mind toward spending as much time as she could manage wrapped under her covers in a sleepy haze. It was the rumblings of her stomach which finally thwarted her. Jonathan was long gone by the time Maggie had tamed her bedraggled hair and pulled on something comfortable that would see her through the day. As such, Maggie ate her belated breakfast alone. The toast had gone cold and stale, but at least Mrs. Doyle had kept the tea warm.

The plate had been reduced to crumbs when a knock sounded at the door. Maggie's brow creased in confusion as she shot a look at the clock. It was too early for her appointment with Walter. She wouldn't have another client for days. Mrs. Doyle was just bustling out of the kitchen when Maggie shot up.

"I'll get it," she said. The housekeeper rolled her eyes as if she were indeed a lost cause. "Camila," Maggie greeted as she opened the door to reveal her standing in the hallway. "Come in. I'm afraid you've missed Jonathan."

A heaviness filled the air between them as Camila slowly removed her coat. "Perhaps that is for the best," Camila said at last. Her full lips were drawn in an unnaturally melancholic turn. There seemed to be a general heaviness to her presence that was so alien to her sunny disposition.

"I do hope you two aren't-"

Camila shook her head to stop her. "I just need some time," she explained. "In any case, I haven't come for your brother. I've come to see if you're alright. I feel terrible that I left you so suddenly yesterday. You were in such a state. I had to come by to check in"

Maggie sank into the settee with a stiff sigh as Camila took a more graceful seat beside her.

"I simply wasn't expecting that to happen. I've never lost control in that way, certainly not in public, surrounded by a dozen or more people," Maggie said. "I wasn't prepared."

"Maggie," Camila said carefully. "I've sat in with you many times now, but that- It was very different. You looked like you were in terrible pain, like you couldn't breathe."

Maggie shuffled. "I am fine now. It was only a memory anyhow. It wasn't real."

Camila's eyes leveled with hers. "It looked real, Maggie. I was terrified for you."

"And quite needlessly." Her attempt at flippancy came out lamely.

Camila raised her eyebrows in disbelief, but let the subject drop.

"I can assure you the evening I had to endure afterward was a far more painful affair."

"You had an engagement," Camila recalled.

Maggie sighed dramatically. "Honestly, Camila. I have never met a man more skilled in the art of conversation in my life."

"He can't have been that bad," Camila said.

"I barely got a word in edgewise all evening!"

"There are worse things."

"Well, if I chose him, I'd be recusing myself to a vow of silence, which simply won't do."

"There is no rush, Maggie," Camila said. "Another will come along."

"Sooner rather than later," Maggie scoffed.

"What does that mean?"

Maggie paused, considering for a moment before she explained. "My parents wrote me just after your engagement party. If I'm not engaged by the wedding, I'll have to move back home."

"You can't be serious," Camila said, aghast.

"I assure you I am," she said bitterly.

Maggie waited, watching as Camila's mind reeled. "Have you written to Charles?"

The words collided with her knocking the sense clean out of her head. Of all the things she had expected her to say-

"Why would I?" Maggie stammered as she recovered.

"I would just think he would want to know," Camila said simply.

Maggie stood. "He left because he wasn't ready to begin an… attachment between us," she explained, her tone ranging from firm to manic as she strode to the bar and poured a brandy, the liquid sloshing chaotically into the glass.

"It's a bit early, don't you think?"

Maggie took a large sip. "It's a bit early for this conversation," she grumbled.

"Maggie, I don't understand. Is there something I don't know?" she asked as Maggie settled back into the settee.

She took another purposeful drink. Her lips parted with an audible click of her tongue. "Charles is not in Virginia."

"What?" Camila said, straightening.

"He's in France, or he will be soon. I'm not quite sure."

"What!" Her eyes widened in violent alarm. "You mean he's-"

"Enlisted, yes," Maggie said. The brandy splashed in her glass as she gestured carelessly. "Apparently, even fighting in the bloody awful trenches of Europe is preferential to being with me." It was a gross mistelling of the true situation. She knew that, but she was also just hurt enough not to care too much for being generous or reasonable.

"Maggie, my God," Camila said in a hollow voice. "But don't you think if he knew your parents were pressuring you to marry, he wouldn't want you to-" Camila stopped herself. "Will you do it?"

Maggie shrugged, laughing angrily. "What choice do I have, Camila!" she shouted, feeling shamelessly unapologetic. "I can either marry here, or they will force me home and then promptly down the aisle with the first eligible man they can find to take me. Now that Jonathan is getting married, I'm just a loose end. They want to tie me up, to be rid of me, make me my husband's problem!"

Camila's face was twisted in shock, pity, maybe even concern, but her response was stolen by a knock at the door. Their attentions flicked toward the sound as Mrs. Doyle came from the kitchens to answer it.

"Are you well, Ms. Ward?" she asked before opening the door.

"Perfectly," Maggie said sourly.

Walter stood in the hall, clutching his hat rather tightly in hand. It was clear by his sheepish expression that he had heard her outburst, though how much was impossible to say.

"Walter," Maggie said, her tone more strained than she had hoped. "I will be with you upstairs shortly."

"Certainly," he said, excusing himself with a nod and making his way up the steps to the parlor.

Maggie took a final sip of her drink and set it down on the little table more forcefully than she had intended.

"I'll come by soon," Camila promised, drawing her into a tight hug.

Maggie only nodded.

She saw Camila out, who parted with a last pained smile before taking to the street. Maggie huffed a deep sigh, alone in the hallway, before turning her gaze upstairs. She trudged up the steps. The door had been left open. Walter was waiting, his bag resting on the table. He'd been cleaning his glasses with a handkerchief, but replaced them as she entered. The table was still littered with articles, though the floor was no longer scattered with paper scraps.

"So sorry to keep you waiting," Maggie apologised.

"It was no trouble. You had company."

"Yes, I wasn't expecting a visitor this morning," she explained. "She was just checking in."

"Are you unwell?" Walter asked.

"What?" If one more person asked her that, she would start taking it personally.

"You said she was checking in on you. I was simply curious as to why," Walter explained.

"Oh, yes. Well, that is a matter I was hoping to discuss with you," Maggie said. "Shall we sit?"

Walter took a seat opposite her, looking through his wire glasses at her expectantly.

"Yesterday, Camila and I were arrested at a rally-"

"Goodness, whatever for?"

"Being loud and controversial too close to city hall, I would think."

Walter grimaced sympathetically. "I see."

"But that is not the essence of my story," Maggie said, waving the topic away. "While we were there, I saw something on an officer's desk. It was a necklace, an ordinary piece of costume jewelry, but I could feel a presence around it. It was like the feeling of the Blackbourne house. Obviously not so extreme, but a spirit was clearly attached to it in the same manner."

"Attached to the object?" Walter said, pulling out a notebook. "Can you describe the sensation as best as you can?"

"Well, ordinarily, when I reach for the void, I feel the queer cold sensation. I can sense countless voices all together. If I have a person or object familiar to a spirit to draw them out, I can generally focus on their singular presence. But in this instance, the chill surrounded this particular object. It grew as I came closer, and I felt only one voice, if you will."

"What happened then? Did you make contact?"

"I did. The moment I touched the necklace, the spirit latched onto me."

"In the same fashion as Anne's spirit, without your consent?" Walter asked, not looking up from his notes as he continued to write in small, tidy print.

Maggie nodded. "And like her, I witnessed her death. Like Katherine, I felt everything… She was strangled."

"Good lord." Walter stopped writing to glance up at her.

"I couldn't breathe, and no one was there to tether me. I couldn't stop it... Her fear was too much..."

"How did it end?"

"There was an officer- I must have grabbed him. I was able to pull myself out then."

Walter nodded. "How are you feeling now?"

"Perfectly well, that's not the point," Maggie said quickly, pulling her focus back to the true point of interest. "The man who killed her- He is the same one who killed those other two women. I'm sure of it. And as far as I know, the police have no idea."

He sat back and blew out a breath. "Unfortunately, your findings are hardly admissible as court evidence."

"Yes, but still, we should try to tell them. It could still help them catch the man. Then they can try him for the others, isn't that right?"

"I don't claim to be the most knowledgeable about such things, but I should think so."

"Ms. Ward." Mrs. Doyle's sharp whisper stole her attention to where she hovered in the doorway. "There is an officer in the hall asking for you."

Maggie looked to Walter in surprise, whose expression seemed to concur that the happenstance was uncanny, to say the least.

"Well, isn't that marvellous," Maggie said irreverently. "Send him up."

Mrs. Doyle eyed her scandalously before turning on her heel, smoothing her hands on her apron as she descended the stairs. When she was out of sight, Maggie exchanged a nervous look with Walter. She couldn't think what had drawn the police to seek her out.

Maggie shouldn't have been surprised in the slightest that it was the same officer she had seen just after she collapsed, Officer Mulligan. He was dressed in the same uniform, a dark blue wool coat with brass buttons trailing down from the chest. His hat was tucked under his arm. Maggie stood to greet him, and Walter quickly followed suit.

The officer crossed the threshold of her parlor slowly, his keen gaze taking in the odd assortment of antiquities and curiosities. However, the peculiarity of it all did not faze him for long.

"Ms. Margaret Ward?" he asked, focusing solely on her.

"Yes," Maggie said. "This is my associate, Mr. Davies."

"Officer Harry Mulligan," he introduced as he shook Walter's hand. His blue eyes flickered between them both, much too exactly to be casual.

"Why don't you take a seat?" Maggie offered as she sat back down at the table.

"Thank you," Harry said, though the air about him remained guarded and uneasy.

"Is there anything we can help you with, officer?" Maggie asked.

"We met yesterday at the station," Harry said. She could not help but notice his eyes quickly grazing the articles strewn across the table.

"I remember."

"You were in a state."

"I was," Maggie admitted, "but I am quite well now."

"I also noticed you'd been through the files on my desk."

So it was his desk then. Maggie stored that away and straightened. "Maybe they scattered when I fell," she lied easily.

To his credit, Harry didn't miss a beat. "How d'you know Ivy Shutler?"

"Who?" Maggie asked earnestly.

"I've never heard the name," Walter added.

"Ms. Ivy Shutler, a prostitute found dead in her apartment by the East River in January," Harry clarified, eyeing them intently.

A chill gripped her throat as Maggie fought to keep the memory at bay. "I never met her," she managed. "But I know who killed her."

Harry waited for her to go on, sitting back in his chair. Yet his shoulders were squared in such a way, making even this subdued posture seem only a shade shy of intimidating.

"It was the man from the papers, the one who killed Katherine Read and Mary Foster," Maggie said.

"Was it now?" Harry said, shoulders sinking as he leaned forward, putting his weight onto his knees. "How d'you know something like that?"

Maggie fumbled, but in her place, Walter explained. "Ms. Ward is a certified medium. My organisation has been partnering with her to advance our psychical research for some months now. Over that time, I have seen her prove her talents time and again."

"You're a psychic?" Harry said scathingly.

"A medium, Officer Mulligan," Maggie affirmed. "I know who killed them because I witnessed it, their final moments through their own eyes. I saw him kill."

"You saw him?" he asked, his expression becoming impartial once more, guarded and unreadable.

Maggie dug through the papers and produced the sketch, slapping the paper on the table and sliding it before him.

Harry studied it for a moment before folding the sketch and putting it into the pocket of his uniform as he stood. "Ms. Ward, I can assure you New York's finest are after the killer of Ms. Read and Ms. Foster. We have a suspect of interest that we are pursuin' now. I can tell you, he does not resemble your sketch. It is my task to find Ivy's killer, and if you have any information-"

"Then they are following the wrong man," Maggie insisted, going to her feet. She still had to look up a touch to meet his eye, but this was far more satisfying than sitting as he towered over her. "If you are really looking for Ivy's killer, I've just handed him to you."

He paused, his jaw setting beneath his cheek. "There is nothing substantial linkin' the death of Ms. Shutler to the others. I would advise-"

"When he strangled her, her necklace cut into her neck. She clawed his arm, trying to get free," Maggie said loudly because it needed to be heard. "The wallpaper had flowers on it. It was water damaged and peeling. Her bed was damp from the leak in the corner-"

"Are ya tryin' to shock me?" Harry yelled, stopping her in her tracks. In his anger, the Irish qualities of his voice grew more potent than before. "I saw the poor girl's body myself! Everything you've said ya could have seen on my desk or bloody well guessed."

"I'm trying to help you!" Maggie growled, undaunted, even as his skin reddened.

"The last thing we need is some broad who reads too many papers makin' up stories for attention," he said, before turning sharply toward the door.

Maggie watched him leave, her teeth grinding together in anger.

"You did all you could," Walter assured, coming to her side.

She shook her head, storming out the door with long, purposeful steps. Below her, Harry was just about to open the door to the street.

"He'll kill again!" Maggie called savagely down the stairs. "You find me when he does."

Harry's blue eyes cast her a fiery stare as he swung the door open. The glass shuddered as he slammed it shut behind him.

CHAPTER

8

IVY SHUTLER DIED IN HER APARTMENT overlooking the East River on January 12th of 1917, information Harry had so graciously provided during his brief visit. It had taken Maggie all of twenty four hours to look up the article about Ivy's death in the city records. Though even that had taken longer than it should have. The poor girl's death was a footnote. Whereas Katherine had made the front page before her murder had even been connected to any larger happenstance. Maggie glanced over the paper of January the 12th twice before she found the mention. The scant article had barely provided any detail whatsoever. However, it did include the one thing she needed, the name, and thus the location, of Ivy's former building.

Maggie walked down the unfamiliar streets in search of the address. Around her the tenements towered, smashed together without an inch to breathe, an impenetrable wall. Laundry hung crisscrossed on every level. Overhead, a woman was beating carpets over the metal railings as a pair of men on the floor above stood talking and smoking cheap cigarettes. The street was lined with carts and stalls, filled with people perusing unappealing produce. It was certainly a side of the city which Maggie had not seen. Jonathan would have fainted at the first whiff of this place, but Maggie was much too determined to let any such thing sway her.

Again she recited the logic which had brought her to this place. The killer had surprised Katherine, and presumably Mary, in the street. Minutes later, they were dead in an alley. Were they random targets? Did he even know where they lived? But before them, he strangled Ivy in her apartment. Not stabbed, he strangled. In the countless hours she had stayed up the night before, she had drawn two conclusions from this. Either he knew where she lived, or she trusted him enough to let him up. Not too surprising given her profession, but still. Second, she had come to the conclusion that he had not planned to kill Ivy. Katherine and Mary had been planned, every detail a conscious choice, and he had chosen to bring a knife. Ivy, he had killed on a whim, without a weapon, just rage... That's what had been in his face in that memory... rage.

Maggie righted herself before the chill took hold.

All of this led her to her new mission. If the killer had not planned to kill Ivy, then he wouldn't have taken steps not to be recognised beforehand, and he had likely not had a thorough exit strategy either. Someone had seen him. Someone would recognise the new sketch she had made and give her something to go on, maybe even a name.

Maggie marshalled her courage and stepped inside Ivy's building. The hall was tiny, taken up wholly by the stacked staircase leading to the many floors above. The smell of waste and rot choked her. On either side were doors leading to opposite apartments. One of them was open wide. The sound of a crying infant echoed into the hall over a woman's voice spewing out fluent German.

Maggie stepped toward the open door and knocked softly on the frame. Inside was a wireframe bed where two young children were playing. Their clothing was either too large or too small and all rather dirty. Tucked away in the back was a kitchen table. The minuscule apartment featured an old iron stove where a grown woman stood over a large steaming pot, speaking rapidly to no one in particular. Sandwiched in the middle of it all was a bassinet. Maggie could see the infant's little arms as it cried. The apartment had barely enough room for another human being to stand.

"Excuse me, ma'am," Maggie said loudly enough to be heard.

"Was willst du?" she asked. Agitation was clear in her expression as she wiped her hands on her already stained apron and picking up the baby.

"Do you know Ivy Shutler?" Maggie asked.

The woman answered... in German, of which Maggie hardly caught more than a word or two.

Maggie dug out the sketch of the killer's face. "Have you seen this man?"

The woman shook her head, waving her off as she went to close the door in her face.

A heavy sigh left her as Maggie turned and knocked on the door across the hall. Nothing. Maggie knocked again and had nearly decided to move on when she heard movement on the other side.

A young man opened the door. He was half dressed in coal stained trousers, his chest completely bare. A rolled cigarette hung from his mouth. His black hair was mussed as if he had just woken.

They both paused, taking in the appearance of the other. Maggie had worn what she had thought would be something rather nondescript for her sleuthing endeavors, but as it turned out, simply wearing well fitting, clean clothes was anomaly enough in a place like this.

After a beat, Maggie recovered herself. "Hello, sir. Do you know Ivy Shutler, the woman who used to live in this building?"

He nodded. "Eh, prostytutka."

Well, that wasn't German. Polish perhaps? Maggie faltered. Was this going to be a recurring issue? How was she supposed to know if they had seen anything? She only spoke passable French and enough Italian to fill an aria, neither of which had she practiced since finishing school.

The young man took a long drag on his cigarette.

Maggie took out the sketch. "Have you seen this man?"

He took it out of her hands and looked it over, exhaling a thoughtful puff of smoke. After a moment, he shook his head and handed it back. Little black smudges lingered on the edges of the paper where he'd gripped it.

"Czy to twoja ukochana?" he asked with a smirk.

"I'm sorry," Maggie said unhelpfully, tucking the paper away.

She was keenly aware of his eyes following her as she went upstairs.

The second and third floors provided as little help. Of the four apartments, only one had spoken English, a gruff old man who'd been no help at all. Another had just shouted in German until Maggie took the meaning and moved on. One family, speaking Spanish from her guess, had produced a young boy, perhaps twelve years old, who had acted as translator. Still, it had provided nothing useful.

Maggie reached the fourth floor, feeling woefully disheartened. That is until she caught a glimpse of familiar floral wallpaper through a cracked doorway. There were four doors on this floor, leading to even smaller apartments... Which would concur with her vision. At the time, she had thought it was a bedroom, but she'd never seen what was on the other side of the door. Maggie stepped closer, peering into the narrow slit. It was Ivy's apartment. She was sure of it.

Maggie strode purposefully to the door and knocked, trying not to look unduly excited. A woman appeared on the other side looking her over apprehensively. Through the thin opening,

Maggie could see just enough to know she was wearing a colorful eastern dressing gown over nothing but her shift.

"Hello, I'd like to speak with you," Maggie said. "It will only be a moment."

"I do not want to talk to you," she said with a thick accent, perhaps Russian?

Maggie shut her eyes, silently grateful to hear the English language.

"Did you know Ivy Shutler?" Maggie asked.

"I knew her," she said, still defensive, but she hadn't shut the door. Her pale blue eyes flicked over Maggie's shoulder, looking out into the hall.

"I'm trying to find the man who killed her."

She studied Maggie again with a furrowed brow.

"Why?"

"Because he'll kill again." They locked eyes for a moment before she opened the door wider and rushed Maggie inside.

Her hair was a pale blonde, tied in a loose braid over her shoulder. She pushed it aside as she tied her dressing gown shut.

Everything about the room was exactly as Maggie remembered it. The water stained wallpaper, the battered dresser in the corner beside the tarnished mirror. Even the bed where the blonde woman took a seat... The bed where Ivy died. Maggie shut her eyes tight, pulling herself back into the present. She was too close to something to fail now.

"Thank you for speaking with me," Maggie said. "I'm Maggie Barlow." She introduced herself with her alias, not out of dishonesty but for practical safety.

"I am Karina," she said, then she paused, narrowing her eyes. "Barlow? You are from the paper! Vy ekstrasens! Psychic, yes?"

Maggie blinked, taken aback. "I am a medium, yes. I can speak with the deceased."

"You have spoken to Ivy?" Her entire body seemed tense to hear her answer.

"In a way, yes," Maggie sighed. "I need to show you a picture. Tell me if you have seen this man."

Maggie unfolded the paper, scarcely breathing as the woman looked it over intently.

"This could be Watchie," Karina said slowly. "He looks different here... more angry, more serious."

"Who?" Maggie asked.

"Watchie was a regular." She saw Maggie's confused expression and explained, "Sometimes we make up names for them, to keep them all straight in our heads. They always give the same fake names, like John or Tom. They all blend together after a while."

"What name did he give?"

Karina's brow wrinkled in thought.

"Why did you call him Watchie?" Maggie asked, desperate for anything that might lead her closer.

"Ivy came up with it. He liked her best. She said he would watch her on the street for hours sometimes, watching her with other men. It's what he liked, I guess," Karina explained with a shrug. "He had a watch too, I remember. He used to check it all the time, like he was late for something."

"Can you think of anything else? When was the last time you saw him?"

"He hasn't been around since Ivy..." Her eyes widened. "You think he killed her?"

Maggie just looked back at her with a solemn expression.

Karina shook her head. "He was quiet, very shy."

Just as she was about to open her mouth to say something else, the door flew open, and her jaw clamped shut. A tall, burly man stood in the doorway. His shirt was rolled up to show the sinuous muscles beneath.

Karina was clearly startled by his appearance. Maggie's own heart skipped a beat, though she composed herself the best she could to hide her fear. The weight of her purse was like lead at her side as Maggie's thoughts immediately shifted to the gun she had stowed within. She had taken the weapon from Jonathan's desk before leaving the house in an abundance of caution. There was a killer on the loose, after all. At this moment, Maggie was very glad she had. The only question remained: if this man decided to charge, would she have the time to draw it?

"Thank you, Karina," Maggie said evenly.

Karina's eyes flickered to her, and she nodded quickly. Maggie forced herself to take one step and then another toward the door, which was still filled almost to its entirety by the large man's frame. He still had not broken his stare. Maggie stopped just before him, close enough to smell the odor of cigar smoke that was steeped into his clothes.

"Excuse me," Maggie said, folding her hands properly before her to keep them from shaking, her purse clutched tightly within them.

He took in a long breath, his chest swelling enormously as he lingered a moment longer. It was a clear message: if she left now, it was at his mercy. Maggie gritted her teeth. At last, he stood aside just enough for her to pass.

"It was Howard," Karina called behind her.

Maggie could have sunken in relief at her words, but she did not hesitate. Instead, she slithered through the opening, their bodies only inches apart as she rounded the hall. A triumphant fire kindled within her as she took down the stairs. She had his face, now his name.

Her mind was abuzz as Maggie stepped out onto the street, planning her next steps. It could only be a matter of time before she found him. Yet, finding a single Howard could still offer its share of challenges in a city of millions. One could check the public records, of course, call on them one by one until she recognised him. But how long would that take?

Maggie was so deep in her thoughts that it took longer than it should have to realise that she was being followed. She had left the busy market streets behind. Now, only casual foot traffic passed by, making the brawny man who had interrupted her in Karina's apartment more apparent as he followed her around the street corner. She was still in the heart of the Lower East Side, not a cab in sight. Her heart beat faster, her hand finding the gun in her purse and clutching it tight.

She chanced a nervous look over her shoulder. He was gone. Her eyes scanned the streets, but she did not see him anywhere. Had she really seen him at all?

Maggie rubbed her brow tiredly. She hadn't slept well, not in days. Her mind could very well be playing tricks. Maybe she should try to rest when she got home. She set her focus on putting one foot after another on the sidewalk.

A large hand gripped her by the elbow, tugging her into a thin alley between two shops. She hadn't even realised there was a space here as she had been walking by, a perfect place to lie in wait. It wasn't until he had pushed her against the damp brick wall that Maggie saw his face. It had not been her imagination, after all. He stood several inches over her, at least twice her weight, most of it in muscle.

At once, Maggie drew the revolver from her bag. His face twisted into furious anger as he grabbed for her wrist. They struggled for only a second, but that was long enough for Maggie to squeeze the trigger. The gun fired, and Maggie saw the impact of it move through his body. He growled in pain and fury. In the next second, he squeezed her wrist painfully enough that the weapon fell from her limp grip onto the ground. He'd been shot in the leg, grazed it seemed. Nothing too serious, though the blood was spreading over his pant leg.

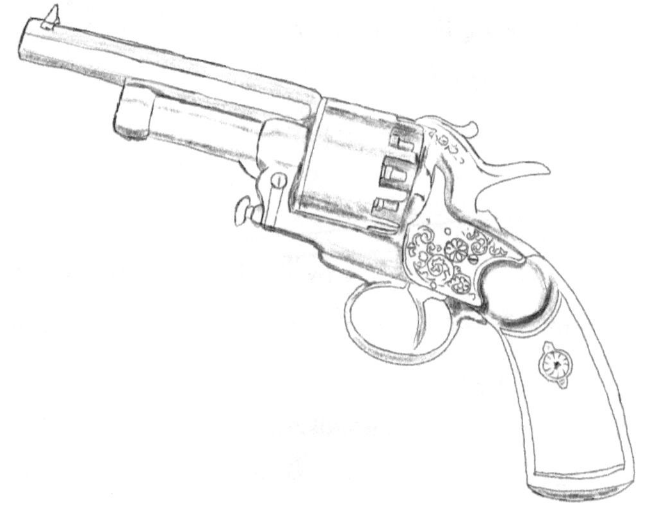

"Ya vypotroshu tebya," he gritted out, drawing a knife from his pocket.

Maggie froze in terror. Her mind split between the pain of Katherine's death: the feeling of the knife plunging into her gut and the thundering of her own heart awaiting the same. Ice filled her veins, clouded her mind. The void was gripping her, and she was too frightened to stop it.

In a final moment of desperation, Maggie gripped the arm that was tight around her wrist. He was too shocked to stop her.

As the darkness closed in, she pulled him down with her.

Katherine's familiar presence drifted near her. She could sense her fear, the pain as she fell weakly into the snow. But she did not allow a connection. No, her focus was elsewhere. The man's spirit was struggling against her. His heart pounded rapidly in her grasp, struggling to be free. It did not belong here, and it was as if the darkness itself was trying to expel him. The force of it was too strong to deny, and soon he was wrenched from her grasp.

Maggie collided back into herself, so suddenly she gasped. She was kneeling on the ground, body shivering, still clasping the man's arm as his body shook violently in her grasp like a fish out of water. She released her hold and stood away until her back was once again pressed against the brick wall. His body stopped shaking, and it was clear that he was alive. Maggie watched frozen as he struggled to stand, groaning at every small movement. At last, he brought himself to his feet, limping on his bloodied leg.

A whistle sounded across the street before Maggie could wonder what he would do next. A policeman was crossing with a deliberate stride toward them. The gunshot, Maggie thought. He must have heard it. She turned back toward her companion. His eyes were locked on her, filled with fear and outrage. The potent mixture stole her breath away before he turned and ducked around the alleyway and out of sight.

"Ma'am, are you-" His words stopped in their tracks as Maggie turned toward the familiar voice. Harry looked at her now in vexed disbelief. She hadn't recognised him from a distance, not in all the excitement. His chest was still heaving from the run.

"Have you lost yer mind?" Harry hissed, pushing his dark auburn hair back out of his face and fixing his hat to hold it in place.

"No," Maggie managed, her tone not as sharp as she had hoped.

"I heard a gunshot," he posed.

"That man pulled me into an alley, so I shot at him," Maggie explained, picking the gun out of the trash pile where it had fallen and replacing it in her bag. It all sounded so fantastical now. "I think it hurt his leg, but not so badly. Though I suppose that much is obvious," Maggie added, looking after where he'd run off.

Harry blew out a breath of exasperation, fixing his hands on his hips. "What in the hell were you thinkin'?"

"What?" Maggie said defensively.

"You're a little far from home, don't ya think?"

"Is that a crime?" Her brow arched in challenge.

"Don't think I'm not on to you," he said, stepping closer. "This is three blocks from Ivy's buildin', and that-" Harry jabbed his finger down the alley. "-was her pimp. From where I'm standin', you're either making yer own investigation into things, or you're involved in this."

"Involved?" Maggie repeated scathingly.

Harry didn't break his heavy stare.

"I'm just trying to find this killer because it seems that the police are content to chase their own tales," she said icily.

His eyes narrowed. "You don't know what you're doin'. You're going to get yourself killed."

Maggie's jaw fixed stubbornly.

"I'm takin' you home."

"I'm perfectly capable-"

"Either I take ya home, or I take you into the station for possession of a deadly weapon," Harry said, taking her wrist.

At once, a flood of warmth spread over her body. Her eyes widened as his narrowed in a curious expression. Finally, he let her go, and the sensation receded. Maggie couldn't help the desire to reach out and touch him again… What was it about him that made his touch so warm, so full of life? She remembered their first meeting at the station. She'd been able to lift herself out of the nightmare of Ivy's death so easily the moment she grabbed his arm. It was like his presence repelled the chill of the Nether…

"Come on," he said quietly, pulling her from her thoughts.

They did not speak for a long while as Harry led her through the streets. He seemed to follow their twists and turns without a second thought, as if he knew them like an old friend. That is until he came to a stop. Harry had led her to a broader, busier road. Cars passed with regularity by the busy shops.

"I am responsible for catchin' Ivy's murderer," Harry said, his tone measured, "and you can trust I'm doing everything I can."

Maggie nodded at the sincerity in his voice. "Ivy's acquaintance, Karina, recognised the sketch I made," she offered, "and she gave me a name." Harry's brows raised in interest, so Maggie went on. "Howard, but Ivy called him *Watchie*. Apparently, he would watch her from the street for hours before..." Maggie's polite language failed her, but Harry offered a sparing nod.

It was clear he was deep in thought as his eyes scanned the road. He raised his arm to hail a passing cab.

"I will find him," Harry said as he held the door open for her.

"I believe you'll try, but that doesn't mean I'll stop looking too," she said, holding his gaze.

He didn't offer any argument as Maggie slid fluidly into the backseat. "320 Warren Street," Harry said to the driver before shutting the door behind her.

CHAPTER 9

MAGGIE PASSED BETWEEN the twin stone lions that flanked the library steps. The sky was clear, allowing the sun to shine freely. Winter was at last releasing its grip as April stretched out before them. Still, as others sat on the steps and walked the streets merrily, unburdened by layers of coats and scarves, Maggie's mind was heavy.

A morning of research had yielded a most disheartening number. Fifteen thousand. The number of Howards believed to reside on the isle of Manhattan alone. She had anticipated a large number, to be sure, but hearing it said aloud. It would not be difficult to find her killer among that haystack. It would be frankly impossible. Even if the world was uncharacteristically merciful and Howard was, in fact, his real name. Karina had said that their visitors often provided pseudonyms.

Maggie hailed a cab. As she settled into the back and offered the driver her address, a dismal question settled into her mind.

Now what? As to that, she had no idea whatsoever. Ivy had been her only tangible lead. She could attempt a sitting to contact Mary Foster, she supposed. Though she hardly wanted to knock on the grieving family's door for their assistance in drawing her out, which would complicate the endeavor. Even so, what could she possibly learn that she hadn't already uncovered? Maggie hardly thought Howard would have bothered to share his home address before killing her.

Her eyes watched Fifth Avenue pass by the window absently. Central Park was crowded with couples and families enjoying the warm spring day. She studied their carefree faces, hands twined together, arms wrapped over shoulders. Their lightness seemed to radiate as evidently as the sunshine. Yet neither seemed to touch her. Inside, she was cold and confused... and alone. When had happiness become just another mystery in her life? It had been such an easy acquaintance before.

Finally, the driver turned toward Warren Street, and Maggie's thoughts turned mercifully with it. Her rather fruitless trip to the library that morning had been spurred on by Camila's appearance at the apartment earlier that day. In all of a second, Maggie had read that she had not come to keep her company but to finally have it out with her brother. So she had excused herself and left them to their own devices. As Maggie paid the fare and stepped onto the sidewalk outside the townhouse, she could only hope that her dear brother hadn't made an even bigger mess of things.

Maggie swung open the apartment door and froze, mouth gaping, utterly powerless to move. The two of them were tangled scandalously over the settee. Jonathan was splayed out, hiding Camila's petite frame almost entirely. All that was visible was her hand gripping the edge of the settee and a leg hooked brazenly over her brother's waist. Maggie thanked any god that was listening that they were both fully clothed.

"Jonathan!" Maggie said as soon as her breath returned.

He shot upright, his flushed face promptly draining of all color. His light brown hair was sticking up at every odd angle, and his shirt was wrinkled chaotically. She hadn't seen this expression of horror on his face since they were children, but the situation had been somewhat different then.

"Maggie!" he hissed at last.

Beside him, Camila peaked over the settee, her hand half covering her expression of mixed guilt and amusement.

"Get out!" Jonathan demanded incredulously.

Maggie nodded abruptly and turned, running up the stairs, forgetting to even shut the front door in her wake. She didn't stop until she was in her parlor. A shiver ran over her body as Maggie shook the image out of her head. At the very least, it seemed they had made up, Maggie thought. A smile tugged on her lips.

It was chased quickly away as the memory of Charles's body pressed against her filled her mind. They had snuck away from the Christmas party to speak in private when he'd kissed her. Maggie's fingers traced over her lips. She had been as she was now, lost, detached, numb to the world… Somehow he'd brought her back. Maggie wrapped her arms around herself as the emptiness of her parlor seemed to swell around her…

"Maggie?" Camila prompted her from the doorway.

Maggie turned, plastering a casual smile on her face. Camila had fixed her thick black hair so that it lay in its usual fashionable curls, though a few treasonous creases remained on her skirts.

"All is well then, I take it?" Maggie asked.

Camila gave a breathy laugh. "Yes, I would say so." She gave another brief smile and took a sharp breath before changing the subject. "Would you be free this afternoon? I have some wedding errands I've been meaning to see to. They'd be so much more agreeable with company."

Maggie hesitated a moment, already exhausted by the idea, before nodding. "Of course."

Within the hour, Maggie found herself on the street once more. Jonathan had offered her nothing more than a grunt in acknowledgement when she told him that she would be going as he hid resolutely behind his paper.

With less than two months until the wedding, nearly all the preparations were laid. Even so, there were plenty of matters that still required their attention. They first stopped by the seamstress, who had finished the latest alterations for Camila's gown. It was an elegant creation of silk overlain with organza. The creamy shade brought out a richness in her warm olive coloring. As ever, it showed Camila's preference for airy fabrics with a ludicrously extravagant train and a veil to rival it. The bodice was simple as not to upstage the exquisite pearl necklace she intended to wear for the ceremony. It was stunning, though not as captivating as the smile that stretched across Camila's face each time she came in for a fitting. Today, she seemed even more radiant than usual. Perhaps it was because the wedding was nearing, or perhaps her brother had just done an exceptional job apologising that morning.

Maggie could not help but feel like an outsider. Normally, she would relish some touch of residual joy at seeing her dear friend so happy. And she was *happy* for them in sentiment. Yet, as Maggie watched Camila's face in the mirror, studying her gown with adoration and... hope, she felt nothing but a sickening twist in the hollow of her chest. She was resolved, however, that her own melancholy would remain as it was: *hers.* It would not be allowed to leech the joy from those she loved. It would certainly not be allowed to mar this day. As such, Maggie sat by, offering compliments and critiques as Camila studied herself in the incalculable reflections of the conflicting mirrors. She rejected her every suggestion that it was too much, telling her the truth, that she looked absolutely stunning.

Camila still made several notes, which the aged seamstress took in stride. Then they were off to the florist, who had three days ago written to tell her it would be impossible to get peonies on the day of the ceremony. Maggie stood back, absently admiring some vibrant lilies while Camila politely twisted the florist's arm until he agreed that, come hell or high waters, she would have spring flowers in the summer.

"Have you seen the church?" Camila asked her as they took to the sidewalk.

"I don't believe so," Maggie said.

"Oh, you must!" Camila said. "We have the loveliest sanctuary for the ceremony."

Maggie smiled with an agreeable nod, even as her heart sank. She just wanted to lay down. But with no apt reason to be as fatigued as she was, Maggie followed Camila on the brief walk up Park Avenue toward the church.

The sanctuary was modest in size, with a simple yet elegant design. The walls were smooth plaster and adorned with tasteful moldings and trim. Wooden pews were lined up in neat rows, facing the focal point of the room, a grand, circular stained glass window set above the altar. The window was a true masterpiece, with each fragment of glass expertly cut and placed to create a mesmerising display of color and light. The shards were richly hued, with deep indigo, scarlet, and sparkling yellow. Sunlight streamed through the window, spilling its colors onto the pews and down the aisle.

"I'm glad that you and Jonathan worked things out," Maggie said earnestly as she took in the sight.

Camila nodded with a smile. "I never truly doubted that we would. I suppose every couple has its hurdles." Her eyes studied the intricate carving of the altar. "We also spoke about you for a time."

Maggie's eyes snapped from the beautiful detail of the stained glass. A spurt of anger rose within her at the idea of being discussed, but she silenced it.

"He's worried about you, and so am I," Camila continued. "You've been gloomy for some time, but lately, you just seem miserable. After everything you told me, the position your parents have put you in, I can understand why."

Maggie couldn't hold back an irritable huff. "What of it?"

"Well, I was wondering what you planned to do about it."

"Do?" Maggie repeated sharply. "What is there for me to do about it? My hands are tied!"

"Honestly, Maggie, I'd never would have thought to see you give in so easily."

"There's nothing for me to fight," Maggie grumbled, setting her gaze back on the pretty window.

"There's always another choice," Camila insisted.

"There's no choice in it at all," Maggie ground out. "You don't understand. Your parents are reasonable human beings! My mother is a tyrant who will stop at nothing to see me married, if that's what she's set her mind on, by the year's end, no doubt."

"Maggie," Camila said softly. "I am sorry that your parents have made you feel like there is no way out of this, but this is your life to live, not theirs."

Maggie turned abruptly. The church was too large, too open. She couldn't stand being so on display. "Camila, thank you for your help, but you simply don't understand the situation."

Camila followed as Maggie stormed the three blocks home in fuming silence. Camila was wrong. Her parents couldn't be swayed, not in this. Her mother's will was a force of nature. If she stood against it, everything would only get worse. She burst through the front door of the apartment, wholeheartedly determined to head straight for her bedroom. However, Jonathan stood as she entered, mouth parting in an expression that halted her in her tracks.

"What is it now?" Maggie asked shortly as Camila entered, shutting the door behind her. The telltale signs of guilt on his face could only mean that he'd gotten word from their parents.

Jonathan cleared his throat. "Mother and Father have written to arrange a meeting in Maryland. We'll meet at the races next week."

Maggie ground her teeth, jaw flaring.

"They've also said," her brother added in a cautious tone that sent a chill over her skin, "Some time afterward, they will be taking up residence in the city."

The rest of the blood drained from her face. "I was supposed to have until after the wedding," Maggie said.

"I'm sure you still do," Camila eased.

Jonathan shook his head. "They've reserved a room for her at the hotel. Mother wants her to stay there until the wedding."

Maggie shook her head. "The moment they're here, she will hardly let me out of her sight. I'll have to stop my business. I'll have to take the advertisement out of the papers. The parlor, we'll have to-" Maggie couldn't even finish the thought before harsh sobs came, forcing her lungs to work as harshly as fireplace bellows. She couldn't go back to that life, her every move watched, managed. A lifeless existence, void of purpose or passion.

Her brother's arms came around her as her troubles spiraled in a whirlwind that stole her air away.

"Just breathe, Maggie," he said, tone steady and soft.

She tried, to breathe in air instead of pure panic. It was several moments before she could. Once Maggie felt somewhat grounded, she found herself being led to the settee.

"We'll think of something," Camila promised, pressing her hand on hers.

Jonathan sighed. "I will try to intercede with them in Maryland," he said. "Besides, we have a week. Perhaps her views will soften before then."

They could all feel the hopelessness of that statement. Though Maggie supposed the fact that her brother would side with her at all over their parents meant something. She only wished it did anything to alleviate the shadow of doom that seemed to be lurking nearer every moment.

CHAPTER
10

IT WAS A HOTTER DAY than Maggie had anticipated when they finally arrived in Maryland. Winter was only just tapering to an end in New York, and Maggie had become accustomed to a damp chill lingering in the air. However, May brought a summer's sun to Baltimore. From the moment Maggie stepped off the train, she had been glad of the wide brimmed hat she had chosen for the occasion. Camila, on the other hand, seemed rather in her element, letting the sun soak right into her bronze toned cheeks with a blissful smile. While the heat might have been a fond reminder to her of her childhood in India, Maggie only felt sticky and tired.

Jonathan called a car from the station to take them straight to the Pimlico Race Course. Their parents had stayed over in the city and would be meeting them in their viewing box. Though idle chatter about the wedding had carried them through the train ride, even that seemed to fail them as they neared the races. Camila had yet to meet her prospective in-laws in person and was clearly experiencing a case of nerves. She occupied herself by fidgeting with her gloves and fixing strands of her hair. After a time, Jonathan took her hand and offered her a reassuring smile that she returned.

Maggie turned, casting her dull gaze out the window, making good use of the small fan she had brought as an afterthought. The streets of Baltimore were in constant motion. Maggie watched a horse drawn carriage pass, the top down, the passengers laughing merrily inside. They passed a family with three young children on the sidewalk, licking ice creams. The youngest had made quite a mess of it.

Soon enough, the splendidly columned entryway of the Pimlico Downs was before them. Their towncar waited in the queue as the other attendees spilled from their vehicles one by one. With every moment, every inch, that drew them closer, Maggie felt as though her stomach was turning to lead. It had been a year since she had actually seen her mother and father. Not terribly surprising really, they had never been the most present of parents. When she was small, they would be gone, often for months at a time, touring Europe or the like. During her years in finishing school, she saw them only on holidays.

The most time she had ever spent in their company was the year and a half after her education was complete. Mrs. Ward decided her daughter required her close attention then. It was a year of dinner parties and cotillions, where Maggie was nothing more than a centerpiece. She had detested every moment of it. Eligible men would come to inspect her as if she were a broodmare. Soon these meetings became a private game to see how outlandish she could be before they would run for the hills. Part of her wondered if her mother hadn't agreed to send her to New York because she had grown tired of it as well, tired of the constant struggle of trying to conform Maggie into a life where she decidedly did not fit. However, any such good luck had clearly run itself out. With Jonathan looking down the aisle, their mother must have gained a new resolve, a second wind.

Maggie blew out a long breath as Jonathan's outstretched hand offered to help her from the car. Again, she was thankful for her own foresight in selecting a thin silk dress, as the fullness of the Baltimore sun beat down on her once more. The pale green underlayer was topped with ivory lace that made up the short sleeves as well, nearly blending into the pale tones of her skin. A rose colored sash finished the dress and matched the flowers which decorated her wide brimmed hat. Beside her, Camila stayed true to her love of airy fabrics with a feather light chiffon gown layered in various tones of blue and green. The outermost layer was beaded with patterns of peacock feathers. A single genuine feather marked her hat, wisping as she turned.

Jonathan escorted them both inside, where the air was filled with excitable chatter and the buzz of electric fans. Maggie followed him straight upstairs to the private box their parents had reserved.

As they approached from behind, Maggie saw her mother's silhouette, straight backed and thin beside her father's broader form. The lace of her gown carried up to her neck, seeming so tight Maggie wondered if she had simply forgone breathing for fashion's sake. Her father was ever as she remembered, though his hair carried more grey than Maggie recalled from their last meeting. Her mother was speaking with another tall, blonde figure. As he turned his face to respond, Maggie recognised his profile at once: Mr. George Cromwell.

"What is he doing here?" Maggie hissed, but Jonathan did not reply.

Maggie's mind was working furiously as they took the final steps before her parents realised they had arrived. It seemed that her mother's tactics had shifted. Instead of sending one bachelor after another, she had chosen to stand behind a single champion.

"Jonathan!" Mrs. Ward greeted with a smile that seemed so foreign on a face made for subtle grimaces and sour sneers.

Their mother took great care in her appearance. Every hair in place, her skin well kept for a woman of her age, but there had always been something about her that kept her from being beautiful. It was all too precise, too refined, if she had to put a finger on it. There was honesty in true beauty, Maggie thought.

Jonathan stepped forward and embraced their mother before giving their father's hand a brief, deliberate shake.

"This must be Camila," Mr. Ward said as if Jonathan was approaching him with a budget proposal, not a fiancée. Their father was every bit the American businessman. A perfect specimen. His manner was direct and imposing, his mustache carefully honed. Maggie had developed a theory in her youth that mustaches were how certain men assessed one another. They would shake hands and stare at each other's lip hair and learn everything they needed to know. If a man could master his own mustache, shaping it into some impressive topiary, surely he could reshape the world.

"It is a pleasure to finally meet you, Mr. Ward, and you, Mrs. Ward," Camila said. "I am so pleased that we will have more time to get to know one another before the wedding."

Traitor, Maggie thought.

"Of course, dear, though Jonathan has written about you so often, it's almost like you're not a stranger at all," Mrs. Ward said, her words sharpened with the thinnest hint of criticism. She turned to Maggie without missing a beat, just when she'd begun to hope she was truly invisible. "Margaret, I'm sure you fondly recall Mr. Cromwell." Her eyes were laced with a cool threat that Maggie could read all too well.

"Of course." Maggie greeted him with a tight lipped smile.

"It is a pleasure to see you again," George said politely. He was wearing a light tan suit that was perfectly cut. His blue eyes were brilliant against the fair coloring. "I had rather hoped that we could meet again after our last dinner ended so abruptly, but your mother informed me that you have been quite unwell."

"Yes," Maggie said, "quite."

"I'm very glad your constitution has returned. When I was young, my sister was often sickly in the winters. My mother had her schooled at home by private tutors. At times, I think it was terribly lonely for her, but we always enjoyed each other's company whenever I returned home. We've always been rather close, being twins."

"Family can be such a comfort," Maggie said, trying to keep the ire from her voice.

"I hope I'm not being too forward, but I have something I would like to show you, if that would be alright?" George asked, looking past her to her mother, who pondered the idea primly before nodding.

With her consent, George turned back to Maggie, extending his arm to her. She had forgotten how wretched this was, to have one's choices stripped away as if she were not a person at all. Maggie could not help but feel like she was being led like the dozens of horses on the track as she took his arm. Certainly, she had a similar level of choice in the matter. Perhaps one day, her mother would see fit to fashion her a bridle, she mused. Maggie sank at the thought. If she could influence it into popular fashion, she most certainly would.

Camila offered her a smile as she passed, which Maggie could not muster herself to return. Mrs. Ward had already descended on her, talking about hotels, seating arrangements, and other formalities that Maggie had been privy to for weeks.

George led her with such confidence that Maggie could only conclude he had been here many times before. The way was accompanied, of course, by his thoughts on the chances of the upcoming race, the recent upset of the Kentucky Derby, and his lamentations that they had arrived just too early to witness the Preakness Stakes.

"I'm glad you've been enjoying your time on our side of the Atlantic," Maggie said when he finally came up for air.

He laughed in an admittedly charming way as they approached the stables. Somehow, the sound only made her mood sink further. Beside them, a groom led out a horse which was being dressed for the impending race. It was a towering giant compared to the ordinary carriage horses to which Maggie was accustomed. Though her father had kept horses, and she had been around them often in her youth, it had been so long that she had forgotten how truly massive the creatures were.

Inside the stable, Maggie was thankful that the horses were tucked safely away in their stalls. Still, even their long faces peering out at them was an impressive visage.

George strolled down the line, pointing out features of interest in each.

"-of course, this being a maiden race, it is hard to pick a favorite, though there is always the matter of parentage to consider."

Maggie nodded as she studied a particularly beautiful black horse in the upcoming stall. Its coat was black as coals, but for where it shined. His chest rose and fell with each breath, full of power.

It was a moment before Maggie realised George was no longer speaking. She looked back at him, hoping he hadn't asked her some question that he expected an answer to. Instead, he was looking at her wantingly. When her gaze met his, he lowered his eyes and smiled almost sheepishly.

"You have a good eye," he said, nodding toward the black horse. "That is Midnight Serendipity. His sire was Polymelus, a true bred English champion, to be sure. His half brother, if you will, won the English Triple Crown just last year."

"How can you possibly tell all that?" Maggie scoffed.

"Well, I should know. I bought him," George said, stepping forward and stroking the horse's long nose. "Would you like to?" he asked, turning to her.

Maggie gave him an uneasy laugh as she stepped forward, raising her hand. Midnight Serendipity reared his head and whinnied, causing them both to startle backward.

"Well, he certainly seems keen to run," Maggie assessed with a nervous laugh. "Hopefully, he will serve you well today."

"Hopefully, he serves *you* well," George said. "He's a gift. I've arranged it all with your father. He's yours."

Maggie looked back at him, speechless. "Oh, George, I couldn't possibly."

"Please, as a gesture of my earnestness, my fondness for you."

The leaden feeling returned to her stomach. Thankfully, Maggie was spared as George looked over her shoulder and then checked his watch.

"Goodness, we should return, or we'll miss the bell," he said quickly.

"Of course."

The stands were filled by the time they returned. Camila was explaining that her parents would be staying at their apartment in the city with her sisters, who would serve as flower girls for the ceremony. However, their talk was interrupted as Maggie and George found their seats once more. Below them, the thoroughbreds were just being led out into the gates.

"There they are!" George said heartily. "That one there is Swift August, if I'm correct."

"Yes, number six," Mr. Ward said, pride swelling. "Sired out of our own stables. Excellent stock. I paid a fortune in stud fees."

"Your Midnight is number five just beside her," George said, leaning in conspiratorially.

Maggie's eyes drifted down. The black horse was pawing in the gates, a bright number five emblazoned on its green saddle blanket. Beside him, her father's horse, Swift August, was a chestnut brown with a black mane and narrow face. The horse seemed to have a less anxious demeanor.

"I have confidence in both of them," George began, speaking to her father again. "The favorite will flare out in the second leg,

I'm sure of it. Though I do believe that Midnight might just possess the speed that will determine such a short race."

This statement launched a hearty debate between the two of them on the merits of American versus English breeding stock. Her father had always described their heritage as that of American royalty, though even he had schooled at Oxford. During which time, he'd made the connections necessary to secure an engagement with her mother, who was born to a prominent English family. Maggie had wondered more than once if there had ever been a spark of any true romance between them. All she had ever seen were comrades working to advance the other's mutual benefit. To all appearances, their pairing may have been as heartless as a simple breeding arrangement.

The bell sounded, and the gates burst open, freeing the horses to shoot forth onto the track at fantastic speeds.

It was hard keeping track of her own, but she found him at the head of the pack at the first turn. Midnight was just behind the two leaders, numbers one and three, which had broken away from the rest. By the second turn, number three was gaining, passing into the lead. Excitement filled the crowd as calls rang out from all around her. Everyone was on their feet in anticipation.

As the horses drove the backstretch to the third turn, the leaders were fading. Midnight was gaining ground until he was at the heels of the number one horse. Swift August was still among the rest of the pack, losing steam as Midnight pressed on, if anything faster than before. On the third turn, he was neck and neck with the leader. Maggie found herself shouting encouragements, anticipation mounting with every heartbeat.

Her heart soared as Midnight Serendipity began to break from the number three horse, charging forward with incredible speed and ironclad determination. Maggie could hardly breathe as he crossed the finish line, winning by three legs. The crowd cheered. She heard the announcers calling out Midnight Serendipity's name and declaring him the winner. A victorious cry sprung from her.

"Congratulations," George said, a wide smile on his face.

The excitement that had jittered under her skin froze. It was the look in his eye, looking to share this moment with her, but more than that, wanting for something she knew she couldn't give. Her manner sobered. Nevertheless, Maggie smiled softly. It was not enough to staunch the disappointment flashing across his features as her enthusiasm ebbed.

"Maggie!" Camila said, wrapping her in a tight hug. "Well done."

"Hardly me," Maggie said, trying to salvage things. "It was George who found him."

She turned back to find that George was already in a heated discussion with her father over the outcomes. Mr. Ward was clearly sore that Swift August had performed so poorly.

In fact, talk of the races carried them all the way from the stands to the country club. It was only after they had seated at their table for lunch, where Maggie had again been sandwiched between

George and her mother, that their conversation turned back to the wedding.

"Now, Camila," Mrs. Ward said. "I have something for you upstairs. It was my grandmother's wedding veil. I think it should do nicely. It's been in the family for generations. It was handmade by her mother for her wedding in 1800 in Oxfordshire, England."

"Oh, how lovely," Camila said politely, though Maggie knew she had already selected a modern veil that she very much intended to wear. "I am very excited for you to see the church. We really do have the most lovely space for the ceremony."

"Yes, I did see that in the paper," Mrs. Ward said, lips pursed. "How are you expecting such a venue to accommodate for all of your guests?"

"I had done a count," Camila said, nodding carefully.

Mrs. Ward shook her head. "We will have to go over it all together once we return to the city, dear. Perhaps The Plaza would be better suited. I can make the necessary arrangements in time, I should think."

"Mother, I'm sure we can find some solution," Jonathan said. "I know how much the church means to her." He gave Camila a reassuring smile, which she returned.

Their mother dabbed her mouth and then offered a false smile. "It can all be discussed later," she said breezily. Translation: *this is not up for discussion.*

"So, Camila, how is it you spend your time?" Mr. Ward asked as he leaned back in his chair, hands resting on a full stomach.

"Well, I volunteer at my chapter of the United Methodist Women, and of course, for the movement as well," Camila said.

"And what movement is that?" Mrs. Ward probed.

"Votes for Women, of course," Camila said. "New York state is on the precipice of the decision, I'm sure of it."

The table was deathly quiet in her wake.

"One must be careful that such matters do not interfere with your duties," Mrs. Ward said placidly, though Maggie could almost hear the sharpening of her knives beneath the table.

"It's just a pass time, Mother," Jonathan said, trying his best to disarm her. "It's good for a woman to occupy her time with such things before she has a family of her own."

Camila shot him a burning look across the table.

"I quite agree," George said, turning to Maggie. "Your brother told me you have your passions. I think it's endearing for a woman to have interests in which to spend her time. Though, of course, the familial duties are paramount," he said with a nod to Mrs. Ward.

"Surely you do not share in such political convictions?" Mrs. Ward said, turning on her fast as an adder. "I would hate to think your time in the city has been ill spent."

"I have accompanied Camila on a number of occasions. I think the cause is honorably progressive and that the ladies who support it do so with great bravery," Maggie said as evenly as possible. Her mother looked at her sourly as her father's jaw clenched. Of course, to them such an opinionated outburst was the height of embarrassment. *Progressive* was as good as a curse.

"I have done everything to make sure their involvement has been entirely proper," Jonathan again attempted to save her, and Camila.

It did little to help. Mrs. Ward simply took a sip of her wine, maintaining her contemptuous expression. Worse, Camila looked as if she would lose her nerve with Jonathan at any moment.

"In any case, Margaret, I think it would be best if you came to stay with us at The Plaza," Mr. Ward said. "Until the wedding, that is."

Maggie felt as though she had swallowed her tongue.

"It seems quite an effort when she'll be moving home in a matter of weeks anyhow," Jonathan said, voice layered with forced nonchalance. "Having her relocate twice seems unnecessary."

Mrs. Ward pursed her lips. "Certainly, you would enjoy the quiet before the wedding."

Maggie remained willfully silent. To show any sign that she wanted to stay now would ruin the entire gambit.

"Of course not. Maggie has been a great help in planning the wedding." Camila came to her aid. "I don't know how I would get on without her."

"Well, now you have me, dear," Mrs. Ward said icily. "We could all visit together."

"Perhaps Jonathan has a point." As George spoke up, Maggie used every tool of composure she possessed to keep the utter shock from registering on her face. "Moving twice seems an awful hassle. I would hate for her to be uncomfortable."

Maggie saw the uncertainty crawl into her mother's eyes, and thus she struck the final blow. "That is very sweet of you," Maggie said, placing her hand on George's gingerly, eyes sparkling.

Mrs. Ward's eyes narrowed ever so slightly. Her champion had turned against her, and to dispute him would be rude. She was cornered in her own game.

"I suppose if it is what your brother would prefer," Mrs. Ward relented. "It will give you more time to prepare."

A weight eased from her chest at this small taste of victory. As the conversation steered to more mundane topics, Maggie shot Jonathan a thankful glance. Though it was clear, at least to her, that Camila was still simmering throughout the meal, as she expertly avoided Jonathan's eye and said no more than was necessary.

When the meal was over, George offered his arm once again. "Might I escort you to the hotel?"

With a quick glance at her parents, Maggie could see this was an agreed upon gesture. She would have accepted with a begrudging spirit had it not been for his earlier intervention. But now curiosity had gripped her, the need to know what had driven him to come to her aid.

"Yes, I would like that," she said, lacing her arm around his own.

George was uncharacteristically quiet as they left the club behind. He called them a car and helped her inside. It was an appreciated gesture, as maneuvering the circumference of her hat through the doorway was a careful procedure. He slid in beside her and gave the driver the address of the hotel.

"Thank you for what you said," Maggie said, waiting to see if he would play coy.

George dipped his head. "Anything for a damsel in distress."

"It is good to know that chivalry isn't dead," she admitted, disarmed by his candid speech.

They were quiet for a time before George motioned for the driver to stop prematurely. "On second thought, I think I could use a breath of fresh air," he said, looking to her.

Maggie nodded.

They stepped out onto the warm Baltimore streets. At least the sun was setting, providing some relief. Still, Maggie unfurled her fan.

"Ms. Ward, would you forgive me if I spoke from the heart?" he said as the car pulled away.

"Absolutely. I always prefer when someone speaks their mind plainly. It seems to me the most efficient way to get anything done."

George smiled down at her. "An admirable mindset, a rather masculine one, but-"

Maggie's jaw clenched angrily until she saw the teasing look in his eye. How was he so different from their last meeting? Had she gotten the wrong impression of him entirely?

He cleared his throat, serious demeanor returning. "I won't pretend that either of us knows the other very well. You certainly seem like a woman of many secrets. In any case, I find myself taken with you."

Maggie's mouth went dry, and for once, she was glad not to be given the chance to respond.

"-I do not mean to suggest that what I feel is love or anything akin, only a desire to get to know you further. Perhaps it is the premonition that such stronger sentiments might be fostered between us if given the chance. Yet, I sense a reticence."

"George, we've only just met."

He nodded obligingly. "And I am sure that our disastrous first meeting has done little to endear me to you. Yet I think we find ourselves in a similar position."

"And what would you imagine that to be?"

"In need of a marriage," George explained. "I am the heir to a large estate, the only male heir. Should something happen to me... It would all be lost, picked apart by distant relations. The likelihood of this has only grown, given the war in Europe. I am on leave now, but I will have to return to my post in the Royal Navy in the fall."

"You would marry to keep the estate in the family?" Maggie said.

He nodded. "I do apologise about going on about my home so earnestly the night we met, but it means a good deal to me."

"I was hardly a pleasure either," Maggie admitted, thinking back to the dismal mood that had carried her through that evening.

A small smile marked his cheek. "Asking you to leave your city, your country, is an enormous request. I suppose I was hoping you would fall in love with my home as much as myself. And it is truly a wondrous place. I know that with time, you would come to love it as I do. Of course, you'd have every comfort." George sighed. "I understand that this is very fast and such a change for you from a life in the city. I wouldn't ask for any answer now, only that you would consider it. Consider *me*." He stopped, and Maggie swallowed.

A rich, handsome man stood before her, one who had proven himself to be respectful and kind. Yet the doors of her heart would not budge, not even an inch to spare her. Yet Maggie made herself nod, forced a smile to her lips.

He must have taken her gesture as a hopeful sign as he smiled back and led her through the doors of the hotel.

CHAPTER

11

NIGHT FELL OVER BALTIMORE. The darkness outside her window was interrupted only by the glow of the street lamps below and the incessant chirping of some unseen population of insects. Late as it was, Maggie had not even attempted to sleep. It would have been an utterly hopeless pursuit. Over the last hours since her *honest* conversation with George, her thoughts had woven into an incomprehensible web in which she was caught in the center.

She did not want to marry, at least not now, but it seemed to be growing into an unavoidable eventuality. What other choice was there? Yet she could not imagine actually marrying George, being shipped off to his English country home. George was a fine enough man, but she did not care for him. And more, New York was her place. It would kill her to leave it. But to refuse George, wouldn't she be forced to leave it anyhow? What other, more objectionable, suitors might her mother force on her once they were back at their family home with no one to back up her interests?

Maggie growled, squeezing her temples. She couldn't be alone with her thoughts another moment, or they would drive her truly insane. Tying her dressing gown shut, Maggie left her suite and strode down the hall to Camila's. Thankfully, at this hour, the rest of the hotel was already in their beds, and she slipped in without being seen.

Camila had not found any rest either, an eventuality Maggie had not even considered, given her own nervous state. She looked up from her vanity stool, looking every bit as spent as Maggie felt. She was wearing an ivory dressing gown embroidered with roses. The sleeves were loose, falling to her elbows as she smoothed some cream into her skin. Maggie let out a rough exhale as she shut the door behind her. Camila's eyes widened in agreement.

"You'll have to forgive me," Camila said.

"Whatever for?" Maggie asked as she found a seat in the chair by the fire.

"All of my advice, it was horribly insensitive. I see that now," she said, looking down at her hands as she worked the last of the lotion into her fingers. "I didn't understand..."

"What I was up against?" Maggie added sorely.

"Precisely," Camila returned with a similar sentiment. They were quiet for a time before she spoke again. "George did seem an ally today."

"Yes, he was," Maggie agreed, though she could see well enough that there was a question beneath the statement. "He's different than I first believed him to be, but that doesn't change a thing."

"Whatever you decide, I'll be behind you."

Surprise left her speechless, staring. "Thank you," Maggie said sincerely.

Camila smiled.

"So, how are you recovering?"

"Whatever do you mean?"

"My mother practically mauled you at dinner," Maggie said, and Camila gave a bitter, knowing laugh. "I, for one, know how unsettling it can be."

"Honestly, I had all these worries about making a good impression," she said thoughtfully. "I should really thank her."

"Thank her!"

Camila looked her dead in the eye. "Nothing I do will ever be good enough for her. It's quite freeing really, not having to worry about it."

Maggie blew out a breath and sank gracelessly back into the chair.

"I just wish-" Camila stopped herself.

"What?"

She sighed. "I wish Jonathan wasn't so keen to seek her approval."

Maggie's lips went tight. "We both learned to handle our parents in our own way," was all she could think to say.

Camila was still pondering her words when she saw the knob of the door begin to turn. Maggie turned toward the sound just in time to see Jonathan's head poking in. It was a second before his eyes travelled the room far enough to see his sister looking back at him scandalously.

"What are you doing here?" he hissed, pulling himself through the door and shutting it behind him. He was still dressed in his dinner clothes, though he had shed his suit coat and vest.

"I should think I have more license to be here than you," Maggie shot back.

Camila sighed. She loved them both, but sometimes they were no better than children. "Maggie, would you mind? We just need a moment to speak."

Maggie looked back at her. "Of course," she said, making her way to the door. She stopped in front of her brother. "But I don't want to hear another word of my *dealings with men*," she added pointedly.

Jonathan reddened, but having made her point, Camila watched as she sauntered through the door, shutting it behind her before he could find his footing in the argument.

"You must admit she has a point," Camila said once they were alone.

"It's entirely different."

Camila eyed him skeptically.

"We're engaged," Jonathan explained.

"We weren't always." Her brow arched in emphasis.

He held her gaze for a moment before relenting with a huff.

"I assume you are here to discuss that travesty of a dinner?" Camila asked, her tone turning somewhat harsher as she changed course.

"I spoke with Mother and Father, and I think you made a rather good impression," Jonathan reassured.

Camila's expression hardened. "It wasn't their approval to which I was referring."

Confusion gathered in his brow, and it was just too much. Camila stood, unable to contain her agitation a moment longer.

"Tell me," Jonathan said.

"Your mother, when she came after me, you should have defended me, or at the very least, let me stand on my own! Instead, you belittled me..."

He looked back at her in bewildered disbelief.

"It's *just a pass time?*" she repeated his words, her voice thin.

"I know your causes are important to you," Jonathan said. "I was only trying to spare you-"

"Are my *causes* just something you tolerate now? Because if you are just waiting for me to settle into some dutiful-"

"I thought we had already settled this?"

"Clearly, we had not reached the understanding I had thought!"

"Camila, darling, I love you. I love how passionate you are-"

"But?" Camila cut in with the word that was obviously meant to follow.

"Can you fault me for being worried? You were arrested, for heaven's sake!" he said, his own temper rising now.

Camila's lips clamped together, and she turned from him, anger and pain twisting dangerously in her chest.

He waited silently, rooted in place.

"You're worried I'll be a bad mother," Camila said. The words refused to escape her as more than a whisper. "You actually think I would neglect our child for my own interests?"

"Darling, no-"

"Isn't that what you're all so afraid of!" she yelled, unable to get a hold of herself.

His eyes widened.

"I will never stop fighting for what I think is right," she continued, her tone measured. "But I would never neglect my family."

Jonathan's hands planted on his hips. His brows were set heavily over his eyes. She could see he was deep in thought and did not interrupt. "No, you wouldn't," he said at last. His voice was tender, soft and heavy all at once.

Camila watched him as he stepped closer, her blood still running hot through her veins. "One might even suggest that the entirety of raising *our* children might not fall solely on my shoulders."

"I'm sorry that I ever made you feel as though I doubted you," he murmured. His large hands spread over her shoulders. "I know that when the time comes, you will be a wonderful mother. And I- I will be a father..." His brow knotted. "I will be present in our children's lives."

"If we are going to do this," Camila said slowly, looking up into his face, "we need to be united."

Jonathan sighed. "I was only trying to protect you. My parents- They have certain expectations..."

Camila reached up, touching his cheek, locking with his blue eyes. "I don't need a protector. I need a partner."

His gaze didn't leave her own as his hand traced up to her cheek. Camila could feel her heart beating throughout her body. As he leaned down, the world narrowed until even the dimly lit hotel disappeared. It was only them.

"I love you," he whispered, his words brushing against her lips.

Camila nodded, touching her forehead to his.

"From now on, it's you and me," he said.

She tilted away, eyes catching his. "You and me," she breathed. "Always."

His hand slid into her loose fallen hair, curling at the roots. Her lips parted as he came to her, slowly, softly. Her breath hitched as his arm wrapped around her waist. A groan vibrated in his chest, sending its shiver through her.

His touch smoothed over the curve of her bottom, reaching down for her thigh. Camila hopped at his cue, hooking her legs around his middle as he lifted her in a single, fluid motion. Jonathan moaned his approval as both of her hands cupped his cheeks, combed through his hair. He held her tight against his body as their kiss grew deeper. His tongue swept over her, and Camila tensed in his arms.

He parted from her with a long, hot sigh. She saw as his eyes flickered to the bed. Within a moment, she was falling onto the feather coverlet, his lips trailing from her neck to her shoulder.

"Jonathan," his name gasped from her lips as his hand found her breast.

At her call, his lips were on her own once more. Feverish euphoria clouded her mind beneath the weight and warmth of his body. They needed to stop, a small voice rose in her mind. They were not married, not yet. It wouldn't be right... Her breath shuddered as his mouth found the tender skin of her neck once more.

Just a minute more...

He kissed her, harsh with finality, as his hands tightened into fists. A tangible emptiness filled the space as Jonathan lifted himself, only inches away, but still far enough for her body to ache for more.

"It's only a few more weeks," he said. She felt the struggle in his voice echo through her whole body.

Jonathan's eyes studied her for a moment, still glazed with desire. She couldn't stand it.

Camila hooked her arm around his neck and kissed him wantingly. His arms came around her, holding her up as he met her passionate embrace.

Too soon, they broke apart, Jonathan pressing his forehead into hers as they let out hot panting breaths.

"We are testing the bounds of my self control," Jonathan said, his tone measured.

A wicked spirit within her reveled in his words. Why not let the fires push them beyond boundaries and reason? She could see it in his eyes. He was on the edge of succumbing to his passions, as was she. All it would take was a single one of them to push...

But he had not pushed her. He had respected her wishes, what she really wanted. Camila swallowed a breath of cool air. Some things were sacred between a husband and a wife. In her heart, she wanted to wait. She knew in the morning she would consider it a mistake if they were to carry on. Camila moved to sit, and Jonathan stepped aside to offer her the space.

"I hope you know that-" Jonathan struggled. "I think you are so beautiful. You're simply perfect, and-" His words failed him.

Camila smiled conspiratorially and stood to meet him. "Our wedding night cannot come soon enough."

His eyes fell on her once more, heady with desire.

Taking in a strengthening breath, Camila turned from him. She sat before her vanity mirror, taking a brush through her now tangled hair.

"Before I go," Jonathan said, his voice still intimately quiet. "I want to know that everything is settled between us."

Camila set down her brush as he came to kneel beside her. Their eyes met for once on an equal plane.

She nodded.

"This wedding, these next weeks, may be a challenge."

Camila reached for his cheek. "As long as we are united, we'll make it through."

He took her hand, inhaling her scent as he brushed his lips over her knuckles. "And then we'll be man and wife."

Camila could not help the wide smile from spreading across her cheeks.

"I suppose I will see you in the morning," Jonathan said slowly.

"I wish you didn't have to go," she whispered. "I just want to be near you."

"I fear if I stay any longer, I won't be able to leave," he sighed earnestly.

Camila nodded. "We will see each other in the morning then."

"Yes," he said with a weak smile. "Good night, darling."

He stood, but hesitated. Jonathan leaned in, giving her one last tender kiss.

CHAPTER

12

WHATEVER HER BROTHER had done last night had clearly been enough to make amends, Maggie thought as she saw them that morning at breakfast. Which was a considerable feat, as she was sure that Camila was more upset about the dinner with their parents than she had cared to let on. Yet any more conjecture about what had occurred after she left Camila's room had been pushed fervently from her mind. There are just certain ways one should never consider one's brother, but it was more than that too...

The feeling had stirred in her chest as they said farewell to their parents. It would only be a brief separation, as they would be taking up residence at The Plaza by the end of the week. Jonathan had stood with Camila's arm looped around his, but not in the casual stance of an escort. Her shoulder was pressed against his arm, his hand on hers in a possessive and utterly endearing way. All the while, Maggie said her goodbyes to George, feeling absolutely no spark of affection whatsoever. Perhaps it would not have ached so much if she did not know how it felt, that heart pounding longing. But as they took the train home, Maggie could hardly stand to look at the pair of them. Her forehead pressed against the unforgiving glass of the window as Camila rested against her brother's shoulder.

Camila departed straight from the station to her apartment, leaving Jonathan and her to make their own way back to Warren Street. Maggie trudged up the steps, perfectly disposed to spend the rest of the day in a melancholy heap. That is, until her eyes grazed the overstuffed mailbox. For months, they had been receiving congratulations from every distant relation and acquaintance, as well as correspondence about other wedding matters. Yet sticking out of the slot now was a newspaper. This was very peculiar because the last two days' papers were lying unread on the doorstep.

She emptied the box as Jonathan opened the front door. Barely aware of her surroundings, Maggie followed him, sifting through the pile. The letters were all for her brother. Maggie tossed them aside on the small table, eyes grazing the newspaper. It was yesterday's, the front page declaring in bold print, KILLER STRIKES AGAIN; POLICE NAME HIM VALENTINE RIPPER. Maggie gripped the paper tighter, eyes skimming the story printed below ...*Eileen Whitcher, age 22... found dead in alleyway... stabbed... note from the killer found on the body... police heard referring to the killer as the Valentine's Ripper, further details declined by officers on the scene ... police working diligently, advise women to take caution in walking alone...*

A note was fastened over the grainy image of the alleyway where the body must have been discovered. It was written in short, messy print.

We should meet. H.M.

Harry Mulligan. Maggie's heart practically stopped.

"Maggie!" Jonathan said, standing only a few feet from her. The clear irritation in his expression told her that this was not his first attempt at getting her attention.

"I have to go," Maggie said, turning on her heel. All travel weariness had left her as she focused on the matter at hand. The killer had struck again, as she knew he would, but still, the present fact of it stoked the urgency within her.

"Go where?" he said, sounding more exasperated than surprised.

Maggie stood for a moment, wondering what to say.

Jonathan just sighed. "You know you're not going to be able to keep this up once they're here."

Maggie's jaw clenched. It wasn't his fault that he was right, but still.

"Just tell me you're not being reckless."

The witty retort stuck in her throat at his unexpected response. "I promise," she said, openning the door wide.

"Wait!" Jonathan called. "Do you have any idea what's happened to the door?"

Maggie turned. She hadn't noticed it before, but the center of the door was splintered rather violently. "I haven't the faintest idea," Maggie said as she studied the damage further. It certainly didn't look like it had been struck by a fist or a rock. The notch was too small and straight for that. Perhaps it had been nicked by someone moving a large piece of furniture? "Ask the neighbors," Maggie dismissed.

He nodded absently, still studying the splinted wood, as Maggie slipped out the door to the street. A nervousness bubbled up inside her as the cab pulled away toward the police station. With all hope, Harry would be working, or else she would have no clue as to where to find him. Still, her thoughts had her fingers tying themselves in knots. Why had he wanted to meet with her? He clearly didn't believe in her abilities and had promptly run her off every time she tried to assist. Had something about this latest murder changed his mind? Or had he seriously begun to consider if she was involved?

Maggie smoothed her brow as the guilt surged over her. She might not be involved, but somehow Eileen's death felt like it was partially her fault. The poor woman had died while she was at a damned horse race. Maybe if she had been here, if her attention wasn't so split... Maggie steeped in this unforgiving spiral of self loathing for the rest of the cab ride.

Soon enough, Maggie was back on the streets. The ground was still wet from the night's rain. Overhead, the sky was overcast and threatened another downpour. She could smell the scent of it in the air. Maggie set a quick pace inside.

Inside, the station was in chaos. Many more of the desks were manned than the last time she had been here, and it was clear as to why. The place was flooded with all manner of nervous looking people. Some were being attended to by the officers, but Maggie found herself facing a rather sizable number who were simply waiting. There were a few seats provided for such a purpose, but not nearly enough.

The desk officer looked up at her with a ragged, belligerent expression. "Miss," he said as she approached. His polite manner was only a thin veil over his obvious exasperation. "If you have no information about the case at hand, please return home. As you can see, we are doing our best to-"

"I'm here to see Officer Mulligan," Maggie cut in before he could finish dismissing her.

He looked her over, his brow settling grumpily. "If this is a personal visit, I'll have to ask you to leave."

Maggie glared back at him. He may be spread thin, but her patience was waning as well. "It's not a personal visit. He's asked to see me," she growled.

"And he can *see* ya after he's done." His every syllable was enunciated as if she were being a troublesome child.

She was about ready to stamp her foot and scream like one too. "It's about the murders. It's important," Maggie bit out.

His expression was distinctly unimpressed.

Enough was really enough. Maggie set her jaw and marched around the desk. If he was going to treat her like some brainless floozy... The rest of her thought was lost to wrathful internal snarling as her fists clenched at her side.

To his credit as an officer, and her great annoyance, the desk officer was only startled by her forwardness for a moment. She had barely made it a few steps before his meaty hand was clamping around her arm.

"Alright, missy," he snarled. "It's home or the lockup. Choose wisely."

Maggie stared him down, seething. "You let go of me." The anger running through her turned cold as ice. Her skin prickled against the sensation.

To her surprise, he recoiled. His brow furrowed, eyes widening.

Maggie stepped back, only then realising what had happened. The veil had touched her in her anger. He had been holding her- Had he felt it? She thought of the man who had attacked her, how he had collapsed. Then Maggie had felt the chill of it in her fear and chosen to pull him down into the darkness. It had been a conscious choice. Was it even possible for that feeling to leak from her unintentionally... In any case, this man had clearly felt something that had startled him.

She straightened, trying to collect her nerves. This was worrisome, to say the least, that somehow she could affect another living person without meaning to. Her abilities had been growing over the past months to be sure, but if this was the cost...

"Ms. Ward?" Harry's voice drew her attention at once. The icy whisperings dissipated from her skin like morning mist against the sunlight.

The officer beside her had apparently recovered from the shock and tried to grab her again. Maggie shook him off peevishly. It was something to be said about the madness of the offices that her altercation with the desk officer had gone almost unnoticed by the others.

"D'you know this lass?" he asked as Harry approached them, dressed in his customary uniform.

"I told you as much," Maggie snapped.

"Yes, sir," Harry said. "Been expecting her."

"You should save your personal visits for after your shift," the more senior officer growled.

Harry removed his uniform hat and combed his fingers through his ruddy brown hair. "Well, that's just fine then. I'm on my way out." When the other officer looked as if he would protest, Harry eyed him steadily. "Been workin' for ten hours straight, Barker." As he mentioned it, Maggie could see the tired shadows below his eyes. "Hardly had time for a shit. Do I need to call the union man?" She couldn't stop her brows from rising at his crude language any more than she could keep herself from respecting his sheer gall.

The desk officer's skin reddened, unhappy with being bested, but he glanced over his shoulder at his post, which was now being overrun. With only a grimace back at them, he took his temper elsewhere.

"Come on," Harry said, nodding for the door.

"Where?" Maggie asked, already following him.

"Just around the corner. Someplace we can talk." His expression hardened a touch, though Maggie did not think it was intentional toward her. Clearly, his mind was heavy. She knew the feeling well enough. It was oddly comforting not to be the only one with a weight behind their eyes.

Harry held the door, but not in the way a man ever had for her. Instead of opening the door from the outside and waiting for her to cross, he opened it and held it from his foot and elbow. Was she so spoiled for noticing the marked difference? Maggie couldn't ignore the closeness as she passed him. He was following her before she was even through the door. The whole exchange was so utterly casual, and so very alien to her.

Maggie had always known that she lived a life of privilege. The comings and goings of the common man or woman were largely unknown to her, mostly because she had never really bothered to explore them. Not that Maggie thought she was better than them, but that their worlds were insular. What opportunity had there been for her to learn, if she was being fair to herself?

Outside, the churning of the skies above chased any higher musings from her mind. Already ominous rolls of thunder warned those below to find shelter. When those clouds burst, it would be a downpour. Harry cut a quick pace down the steps and to the sidewalk. Maggie followed after him eagerly as the first warning flecks began to hit the pavement. One sizable drop landed heavily on her scalp just as Harry pointed ahead. Thankfully, he had not been exaggerating when he said their destination was just around the corner. Maggie followed his gaze to a little pub. The wood surrounding the many windows was painted black. Chipped gold paint over the door read *Mullarkey's Public House.* Her mother would flay her alive for setting one foot in this place. They practically dashed toward the door.

"After you," Harry said a little breathlessly, swinging the door open in his way. God help her if this doorway wasn't narrower than the last one. It was impossible to slither past without the fabric of her coat sliding against his chest.

CHAPTER

13

INSIDE, THE SCENT OF RAIN in the air was replaced with the thick, sweet smell of beer. A rumbling cloud of chatter encircled them as they crossed the threshold. The pub was packed, mostly with men, many, many Irish men, though Maggie was not the only woman among them. Maggie's tailored wool suit was somewhat out of place, and she couldn't help but feel markedly overdressed. As ever, Harry did not hesitate to push forward. She followed him closely so as to not become separated.

"Pat!" Harry called toward the barkeep. "Two pints!"

Pat looked up from behind the bar. He was a large man with thick forearms, balding, but with a thick beard. "Ay! Harry."

His eyes flickered to her at his side. Clearly, he had thoughts about her, but blessedly kept them well enough to himself. Soon enough, he was setting two large, frothing glasses of beer on the bar.

"One for you and the lady. On the house for New York's finest." He gave a small nod of respect.

"Good of ya, Pat," Harry said with a brief smile.

Beers in hand, he finally turned to her. He nodded to an unmanned table, and Maggie followed.

Maggie hiked herself onto the tall bar stool as gracefully as possible, which wasn't very. As she pulled her hands away from the table's surface, she realised it was sticky.

Across from her, Harry let out some kind of snort and slid her beer across the small table.

"What?" Maggie snapped.

"Never really met a lady like you before."

Maggie narrowed her eyes, but he just took a very long drink. She followed suit. Beer had never been a favorite of hers. At finishing school, they had snuck some from the kitchens every so often. The cook kept a secret stash, which was perhaps the worst kept secret at the academy. Still, it clouded her mind with its easing haze and spread a comforting warmth through her body. When she set the pint down, Harry was just staring at her.

"Who the hell are you?" Harry asked. For some unfathomable reason, he sounded frustrated.

"What kind of question is that?" was all she could think of to say.

"Ya don't make a lick of sense," he said, as if that was explanation enough.

"I make perfect sense!" Maggie argued.

He leaned in on the table. "You dress like a lady, and you live in your fancy uptown digs, but I find you wandering the East End askin' about murdered girls?" Harry shook his head. "And you drink beer like my Uncle Hugh."

"I don't see what the beer has to do with anything," Maggie grumbled.

Harry just leaned back, shaking his head as he took another drink. She was sure she saw a glimpse of a smile on his lips.

"Why did you want to talk, Harry?" she asked. He looked at her for a second. "Officer Mulligan," she corrected herself quickly.

"Harry's fine," he said, but then his playful smile faded. His blue eyes bore into her with their exacting stare. "I want to know why an uptown girl is pokin' her nose into these murders and why you think Ivy Shutler's got something to do with it. I want to know why I found a bloody knife stickin' out of your front door yesterday, the day after Eileen was killed."

"A knife?"

Harry raised his brow in emphasis.

"I don't know," she said distantly. Dread pooled in her gut as she thought about the damage to her door. She hadn't given it a second thought since she left Warren Street. Was it possible the killer had left it? What other explanation could there be? Did he know she was investigating him? She supposed it was possible he had seen her at Ivy's building. Wasn't that what Karina said- He liked to watch Ivy? And now she was...

"What about Ivy?" Harry interrupted her thoughts. "And your drawing?" He produced the paper from his coat and smoothed it out on the table. The page was wrinkled and creased as if it had been stowed there for some time. "How d'you come up with that?"

His intensity startled her for a moment, but Maggie collected herself. "I've already answered that," she said lightly, taking another drink of her beer.

Harry nodded exaggeratedly. "You talked to their ghosts."

Maggie's eyes narrowed. "If you thought I was insane, you wouldn't have called me here."

His gaze didn't waver. It was a sudden motion as he lifted his beer and took a long drink. The glass came back down on the table heavily, and he wiped his mouth. "I dunno how you know what you know. And I don't for a second think you have ghosts whisperin' in your ears."

"Then what do you think?" Maggie challenged.

Harry straightened, facing her dead on. "I think that before I even knew your name, I took my case to the Captain," he said, expression hardening, voice going low. "I was talking to a buddy of mine, Shaw. He said his girl, Katherine- He said she was all laid out in that alley, in the snow, like she was asleep. The bastard, he moved her like that on purpose. And I had a feeling it was the same right old bastard as killed Ivy. I felt it in my bones."

"What?" Maggie said breathlessly.

Harry looked back at her. "I was the first one called for Ivy. I've seen a lot of dead girls... Too many dead girls. But Ivy was different from the start…" His eyes were haunted, and Maggie could feel the aching sadness hollowing her own chest. "She'd been tucked into her bed, covers and all. I thought it was a friend of hers or the like, but they said they found her that way."

"The others have been the same?" Maggie asked.

He only nodded.

They had never mentioned that in the papers, and if the killer had really done that, it would have been after… After she would have been able to see. Her mind reeled. What kind of sickness caused a man to kill a girl with the anger she had seen, only to show her kindness in death? Her stomach turned. She was going to be sick…

"Our suspect fell through," Harry said out of nowhere. "I shouldn't be telling ya." He gave her a sideways glance that told her it was eating at him. "God, I was so relieved when the Captain said they had the guy. There was a good connection between Katherine and Mary. They just needed to wait until he put a toe out of line. We were followin' him for over a week. Had our bloody eyes on him when Eileen died."

Maggie finished the dregs of her beer if only to keep herself from uttering a dark *I told you so.*

"The whole station is flooded with people with useless tips. They're scared, and rightly so. Every family that's ever lost a girl is beatin' down our doors." He rubbed his face. "And we've got bloody nothing to tell 'em."

She could feel the full weight of his hopelessness in his voice. "So that makes me a last resort, then?" Maggie surmised gently.

His brows raised humorlessly, and he finished his own drink.

Pat appeared a moment later. "Another round, you two?"

Harry was about to nod as Maggie spoke up. "Two whiskies, please."

They both looked at her as if she had asked for an elephant in a teacup. "Comin' right up," Pat said at last, patting the table as he spoke. She could see his sides shaking as he walked away.

"I have a question," Maggie began. "Why are papers calling him the Valentine Ripper?"

Harry sighed. "There was this note left on Eileen's body. The first guys on the scene were making jokes, idiots. The papers heard 'em."

"What did the note say?"

"He wrote details of Katherine and Mary's death." His fingers traced his lips and then fell heavily to the table, cupping his empty glass. "Threatened to kill again, called it *leaving a Valentine*."

Maggie grimaced. "Katherine was killed on the 14th, wasn't she?"

Harry nodded. "It does seem to be a reference to the first killing. He also taunted the police, hinted that there may be other girls out there..."

"You don't think- Could he be talking about Ivy?"

Harry gave her an affirming glance but said nothing as Pat returned with a pair of whiskey glasses. He grumbled his thanks and tilted his glass back, taking a sharp swig.

"So, what can I do to help?"

The tense expression on his face told enough. He was stuck, and it was killing him, not knowing what to do next. "Is there anything you're not telling me?" Harry said finally, clearly grasping at hope.

"I wouldn't hide anything from you," she said earnestly. "I want him caught as much as anyone."

He just looked at her with an assessing gaze, still deciding if she could be trusted, no doubt.

"I could try reaching out to her," Maggie offered.

He raised his brow.

"Eileen."

His hand rose to rub his face. He muttered something about the saints.

Maggie took a drink.

"What d'you need then," he said, "to do whatever it is you do?"

"Well..." Maggie shuffled. "Usually, I am with a person who was close to the deceased. Their presence draws the spirit out."

Harry blew out an exasperated breath, and Maggie glared at him.

"If you don't-"

"Nah- Nah-" He raised his hands. "Keep going. Please."

Maggie pursed her lips, but he simply stilled, watching her pointedly, a silent promise to behave himself. Her drunken mind betrayed her, fixating on his smoky blue eyes. Maggie sent her gaze down at once to her drink and took a small sip. "-an object, like Ivy's necklace, can work as well. Something that was close to them when they died."

Harry didn't speak, though his mind was clearly sorting through all she had told him. Giving him the space to think, Maggie took another burning sip of the cheap whiskey. The pleasantly warm fog coated her mind.

"I'm not workin' the case," Harry said finally, "not officially. I don't have access to her personal effects. And I couldn't contact the family. The Captain would have my head."

"What if I-"

He shook his head once in dismissal. "I couldn't put the poor folks through it." Something flickered over his features, but it dimmed as he looked at her skeptically.

"What?" Maggie asked.

He hesitated a moment more. "What about her body?"

Maggie's stomach turned, but she refused to show it on her face. Would that work? Every fiber of her being told her yes, it would. If Ivy's necklace could affect her so strongly, she could only imagine the potency of being so close to her actual...

"If it's too much-"

Maggie stopped him with a shake of her head. "I could do it. It would work. She may have even seen something- Give us what we need to catch him." Her jaw drew tight at the thought.

He sat back in his chair, giving her that assessing look again. "Tomorrow?" was all he said.

Maggie nodded. Jonathan's words echoed in her mind. Once her parents were here, she would be too restrained. The sooner, the better. "I'll bring my associate, Mr. Davies," Maggie said. Walter wouldn't miss this chance to further his research, gruesome as the expedition may be. Not to mention, she would hardly begrudge having the assistance.

"Alright then," he emptied his glass, setting it back on the table. "Bottom's up," he said, looking to her.

Maggie's brows rose, but she did. When she set down her glass, he was standing before her, offering a hand.

She looked at him quizzically and then beyond. Maggie had been so absorbed by their talk that she had not noticed that at the other end of the pub, many couples had taken up dancing to fast paced music.

"Are you asking me to dance?"

"High class girl like you knows how, don't you?"

Of course, she knew how to dance. In fact, she was rather spectacular at it, but what they were doing over there had almost no discernable form to speak of. They simply stepped to the quick tempoed music in an ever flowing mob.

"I can- but now? I-"

Harry caught her eye. "You're wound tighter than a spring," he said. "There's no better cure." The sincerity she found in his gaze told her he was speaking from his own experience.

She was wound, as he put it, tighter than he had probably even guessed. Maggie looked out at the dancers, the excitement in their carefree smiles. Ordinarily, she would be rushing onto that dance floor. Yet, as she thought about being among them, sadness just gripped her heart tighter from within. When was the last time she had felt that free, that happy?

Months. It had been months...

...and she was so tired...

...and then she thought of Eileen's body sitting cold and lifeless in some dark room. A shiver went through her. Eileen would never dance or smile or anything ever again. Her life was over, gone...

But mine is not, Maggie thought defiantly. Raising her hand to meet Harry's patient offer, it felt as though her arm were filled with lead instead of bones. Even so, her touch on his palm was featherlight. He gave her a brief satisfied smile, though she could see his exhaustion seeping through. He needed this too. There was something terribly comforting in that. It didn't feel so selfish now.

As the next song began, they joined the crowd. The pairs parted like water to admit them as the music began with its frantic pace. Harry put his hand on her waist as hers settled on his shoulder in some bastardisation of the waltz. Yet any instructor she had ever known would have had a stroke to hear such a comparison. The arms were slack, and instead of a three beat step, they moved to a single beating frenzy. Spinning and stepping until Maggie wasn't even sure which direction she was facing. The hold was much tighter, bodies pressed against bodies. Harry's supporting arm was tight around her for the first rounds as she learned the rhythm, practically carrying her through the steps. But once she found her own footing, his touch loosened.

By the second song, Maggie was breezing through the fast hopping steps as if she'd been doing it all her life. Confident with her movements, Maggie chanced a look up at Harry's face. His smile was wide. The effect of it even touched his eyes. Warmth spread through her. Maggie felt herself grinning broadly in return. Without warning, he lifted their joined arm, and Maggie moved expertly into a smooth spin.

"Yer good at this," he said, raising his voice over the music as she came back into form.

Her grin widened.

Hours poured past like they were nothing. They danced and drank, and the rain continued to hammer against the windows with no sign of stopping.

"I should get ya home," Harry said finally as Maggie finished her pint.

Her brows furrowed for a moment, and then she glanced at the clock over the bar. Panic rammed into her. Jonathan was going to lay an egg.

Harry put a hand on her shoulder. "You alright?"

"Yes," Maggie said, collecting herself. It was difficult through the intoxication that lingered as a lackadaisical fog over her mind.

They stepped outside where the deluge was in full force, a curtain of heavy drops splattering the sidewalk violently. Harry left her waiting beneath the small outcropping over the door as he ventured into the storm to procure a cab. By the time he managed to hail one, he was soaked to the bone. He waved her on eagerly, and Maggie dashed through the downpour and slid into the cab.

"320 Warren Street," Harry said, panting beside her.

They were both absurdly out of breath, as if they'd just run a mile, not just to the street corner. But as the car rolled ahead, the only sounds that filled the cab were their heavy breaths and the thousands of heavy drops pelting against the roof.

"Tomorrow then?" Harry asked, pushing a few dripping locks of hair out of his face. Soaked as it was, his hair was a deep brown, no sign of its reddish hues. His uniform looked more black than blue. "You'll be bringing your partner?"

Maggie nodded. "Where should we meet you?"

"The station."

She ran her fingers through her own hair, trying to dry it a bit, but it was a lost cause.

"You'll be careful, won't you?" Harry asked. "The knife? Nothing's sure, but my bones tell me it was him. If he knows where you live..."

His words fell on her heavily. Yes, there was that small matter, wasn't there...

"I understand," Maggie nodded. Perhaps she should take her parent's offer of relocating to The Plaza... As wretched as that sounded, at least she'd be safe.

"320 Warren Street," the driver said listlessly.

Maggie nodded and pulled out the money to pay him.

"I'll walk you up," Harry said, reaching for the door.

Maggie reached a hand for his arm to stop him. "I can make it on my own," she insisted.

He raised a brow as if to question that.

"My brother is already going to be rather upset at the hour. Seeing you would just make it worse," Maggie said, but added to be clear, "He tends to imagine any man in my company must be... romantically involved."

"Are ya?" he asked.

His question kicked the air clean out of her. "What?"

"Are you *romantically involved?*"

She hadn't expected that, though perhaps she should have. They had just spent the entire night dancing, very closely. Her heart was hammering. What was even the answer to that? She had no real attachment to George, but she had agreed to *try* to consider a life together with him... And then there was Charles, who was an ocean away, but to say that she didn't still hold a certain affection for him would simply be untrue.

"Didn't expect that to be a hard one," Harry said sympathetically. "You don't have to say anything."

Maggie only nodded once in thanks before he slipped out into the thunderous rain and held the door open for her. She slid out quickly to spare him.

"Tomorrow?" he asked before stepping back into the cab. He waited for her answer, rain plastering his hair dark against his brow.

"Tomorrow," Maggie agreed.

Harry nodded and slid into the cover of the cab. She took up the steps to the apartment and into the blissfully warm hall. Once inside, her eyes caught on the splintered door. A shiver ran down her back. Maggie forced her eyes away.

As she opened the door, the purposeful energy that had carried through the day was draining, leaving her cold and wet and utterly exhausted. It was a sweet fatigue though, the kind that held the promise of deep, dreamless sleep.

Unsurprisingly, her brother was seated in his armchair, smoking his pipe. Ordinarily, he would have returned to his office or bed by now. As Maggie took off her damp, heavy coat, she could see he was upset, but for some reason, he was trying to tuck it away.

"It's rather late," he said, seemingly unable to help himself as he set down his pipe and stood.

"Time rather got away from me," she admitted truthfully. "I had not expected that to take so long."

"Where were you?" Jonathan asked. His expression changed as he stepped closer. "You've been drinking?" It was hard to say which was the winning expression on his face, disgust, anger, or all out shock.

"Yes, I had a drink or two," Maggie admitted. Though her mind was certainly touched by the alcohol, she was by no means drunk. She had experienced that sensation only twice in her life and did not care for it in the slightest.

"You smell like you've brought the bar home with you!"

"You're exaggerating."

He huffed. "I want to know where you were, and with whom."

"I met with a police officer as a matter of my work. We went to a public house to talk and had a few drinks together," Maggie explained, choosing her words carefully.

Her brother pressed tense fingers against his brow. "I understand that you feel some need to express your independence. Our parents coming is... upsetting for you-"

"Jonathan," Maggie protested. He was making her sound like some irksome child.

"-but Camila expressed some concern about your... habits, and I defended you, but now I think she may be right."

"Camila said what?" Maggie bit out. It cut deep that she would talk to Jonathan about something like this without bringing it to her first. Weren't they friends? The air she drew in felt suddenly cold and forbidding.

"She's concerned!" Jonathan said. "I'm concerned! You're not yourself, not since Blackbourne-"

Maggie's hair stood on end as icy rage snaked through her veins. "You don't know anything about that," she said in a deadly whisper.

"I know that you haven't been the same since you met him," he said. "You can say what you want, but all I see is a man who came in, toyed with your affections, and left you... like this!"

"You don't know anything!" Maggie shrieked. It was all too much. The outrage and betrayal and powerlessness circled around her. Her chest felt hollow and cold, her skin pricked as a chill spread through her blood with every hastened beat of her heart.

Jonathan looked back at her wide eyed, chest heaving. The breath that left his lips came as a puff of steam. "...Maggie?" his voice tremored.

She felt it, the touch of the darkness spreading through her in her anger. A chill hung over the room, not that of a winter's breeze, but the unnatural absence of warmth that she knew came from only one source. Even the fire beneath the mantle was subdued, as if cowering in her wake. Maggie's eyes rounded as her chest stilled. Her connection to the Nether had escaped her, again... and this time in her own home, and her own brother had been caught in the wave of it.

"Maggie." His voice was frightfully gentle as he took a step forward, reaching to place his hands on her shoulders.

She startled backward, clattering into a table. "Don't- Don't touch me." They stared at each other, frozen for another moment, before she bolted. The way he'd been looking at her... with concern for her yes, but also something more. He'd seen, he'd felt, a new side of her, one she'd tried to keep as far removed from him as possible. The unfamiliarity and fear in his gaze wouldn't leave her, no matter how fast she ran.

Maggie didn't stop until she was safely behind her bedroom door. The veil was whispering in the corner of her senses. The air that filled her lungs was cold and cutting. Try as she might, she could not push the feeling away.

CHAPTER
14

JONATHAN PACED THE LENGTH of the sitting room, running his fingers over the links of his watch chain. The hour was still early, but already, fatigue pressed against his senses. It had been a fitful night, filled with dark and troubled dreams. He could not dispel the image of his sister's face lined in anger against him, nor the unnatural chill that had settled over the room thereafter, the kind that made his heart beat harder in protest. As such, Jonathan was deep in his thoughts when the knock came at the door.

He was upon it in three long legged strides. Mr. Davies nodded to him in silent greeting as he came inside. His brow was drawn low and serious over his round features as he took off his hat and set down that bag of his.

"Thank you for coming," Jonathan said, trying to keep his tone casual, controlled. Despite his efforts, brotherly concern still soaked his words. "I know it was early to call on you."

"I came as soon as the office gave me your message," Walter said seriously. "You said she was feeling unwell?"

Jonathan's hands rested on his hips, his shoulders tense. "There's something wrong with her," he explained. "Something beyond... practical medicine."

"I see," Walter said, straightening his glasses. "Is she resting now?"

Jonathan nodded. "I haven't heard a thing from her since last night." Worry prickled at his skin even as he said the words. "I'll go check in on her."

"Of course."

Walter was left waiting for only a moment before Jonathan came striding from the back of the apartment, his face white. "She's not there." His voice was hoarse and quiet, only to be suddenly overtaken by his resounding call. "Maggie?"

Jonathan's panicked voice reached all the way to the upstairs parlor, where Maggie was flipping through the pages of one of her aged books to surmise its contents. She parted the window dressing and was surprised to see that the sun had fully risen. Unable to find any semblance of rest the night before, she had eventually given up and come upstairs. Busy hands had proven to be far more of a comfort than tossing and turning in her sheets.

Maggie left the book on her table to be dealt with later as she turned for the door. She paused as she reached for the knob, realising she was still in her dressing gown. But there was nothing to be done about it now. She sighed and went down the stairs before her brother had a stroke. Jonathan called her name once more as Maggie came to the front door. It opened before her, and Maggie collided into a definitively male figure, and not her brother.

"Walter?" Maggie said as she recovered. She had meant to send word to him that morning about her upcoming appointment at the police station, but she was sure she hadn't yet. "What are you doing here?"

Behind him, Jonathan's flushed face appeared in the doorway.

"For Christ's sake, Maggie!" he said, obviously flustered. "Get in the house!"

"Gladly," Maggie surrendered. She was no more keen to stand in the hall in her dressing gown than anyone else.

She followed them inside. Jonathan at once took to pacing before the fireplace. One day, that carpet was going to give way if he didn't learn to control his nerves, Maggie thought. One could already see the fading in the rug along his usual trail.

"Did you call him?" Maggie asked.

"Your brother was worried about your health," Walter explained for him.

"My health?" Maggie snapped, but she forced an even breath and relaxed before she turned to her brother. "I understand what happened last night was upsetting, but I assure you I have it perfectly well in hand."

"That is a lie-" Jonathan said in exasperation.

"Why don't you tell me what happened?" Walter said amiably, cutting him off before he could make things worse.

Maggie pressed her fingers to her temples. They both meant the best, she told herself. After a sigh that came as more of a growl, her hands set at her sides. "I am going to get changed," Maggie said. "Then we can discuss… this."

They both nodded their agreement in their own way, and Maggie turned on her heel. She dressed slowly, her mind busy in itself. Jonathan was understandably concerned. He'd only seen a brush of her power once or twice, and it had unsettled him. To feel it for himself must have been something entirely more. It would be a lie to say that she wasn't troubled that it had slipped beyond her control here. She had always tried to keep the line between that life and *her* life distinct and separate. The idea that she might not be in complete control of the boundary was unsettling in the least.

By the time she had pinned her hair, Maggie had resigned herself. Jonathan was simply looking out for her, even if she loathed that he had gone behind her back to do so. Nevertheless, it was time she addressed these… slips of her power. It had happened before, months ago, when she had renounced her practices, but eventually, the brief feelings had subsided. Though in those instances, she had never affected the people around her. Yesterday, she had done so without even meaning to, twice. Maggie took in a breath of resolve. She had avoided this for long enough.

Both of them looked to her the moment she entered the sitting room. Neither had taken a seat in her absence.

"Jonathan, if you wouldn't mind, I'd prefer to discuss this with Mr. Davies alone," Maggie said simply, turning to Walter. "In my parlor?"

Walter nodded even as her brother looked as if he might protest. However, he did not. Perhaps it was enough that she was willing to discuss the matter at all, even if it wasn't with him. Maggie just couldn't imagine herself capable of the vulnerability this conversation would require, were her brother in attendance.

She led the way upstairs. The parlor was in a state of well ordered chaos. Neat piles of the most random objects littered the room. The wardrobe doors were open for once, its contents emptied. Across the room, the books were half sorted into wooden crates.

"What's all this?" Walter asked, dismayed by the upheaval of the once familiar space.

"Packing," Maggie said sourly.

"You don't mean that you're giving up on your-"

Maggie shook her head and raised a hand to stop him. "My parents will be here in a matter of days. Needless to say, they do not know about any of this, nor would I want to change that."

"I see."

"I've already sent correspondence to have my notice taken out of the paper," Maggie said as she moved a stack of books piled on top of one of the chairs to make room for them to sit.

"So," Walter began. "Will you tell me what happened? Your brother looks… unnerved."

Maggie made an agreeable huff as she took a seat at the table, which was piled high with miscellaneous objects yet to be sorted. "To begin, I suppose I should explain that there have been times in the past, when I was upset, I suppose, when I felt touches of the Nether without meaning to. It's only affected myself, brief sensations as if I were trying to reach beyond the boundary, chills on my skin and the like. But I could brush these aside, until recently."

"Has something changed?"

"There was an incident," Maggie began. "I was... attacked." His eyes widened as she had feared they would. "I am unharmed totally, perfectly well. But when I began to feel the fear of being harmed, I felt the darkness stirring around me. I took his arm, and I pushed us over the edge, both of us."

Walter's concern turned to something else. "You took another individual over the boundary into the Nether?"

"In my own self defense," Maggie said slowly, "yes."

Walter stroked his chin, looking troubled.

"It was a matter of instinct," Maggie justified. "I wasn't meaning to be malicious. It was hardly a choice even. I just knew in the moment it was my best means of survival, I suppose."

"And how did the man respond?"

"He collapsed, began shaking. But he recovered rather quickly, I suppose, once I released him."

Walter rubbed his mouth, shuffling in his seat.

"But ever since," she continued, "when I get upset, these feelings come over me, and now they're affecting those around me beyond my control..."

"Your brother said the room became very cold," Walter said, his expression still unreadable.

"Yes."

Walter straightened. "It sounds as if this may be some sort of defense mechanism. Triggered by an inciting incident and prolonged by stress."

"That sounds... feasible. But even if you're right, what would you suggest I do about it?"

He loosed deep breath. "Remove stress, perhaps controlled practice of your abilities in a safe environment over a period of time."

Maggie let out a tense laugh. "I don't think either of those will be possible for the foreseeable future. It is not as if my problems are ones that will be going away any time soon."

Walter made a thoughtful gesture, but said nothing.

"I was actually meaning to send for you today," Maggie said. "Officer Mulligan has agreed to accept our help in the matter of finding the Valentine Murderer, or whatever the papers are calling him these days. He's agreed to accompany us to the morgue so that I can make a connection with the latest victim. I was hoping you would be able to attend."

"Are you sure this is wise?" Walter said. "Perhaps to delay-"

"I can't," Maggie dismissed. "My parents will be here in days. I've decided that I will be staying with them after all. But that means that as far as the investigation, my hands will be tied. Not to mention, the killer is still on the loose. Besides, the matter is rather more pressing than I knew."

"How so?"

Maggie sighed. "Well, it seems that the killer knows where I live and made it a priority to let me know as much. Thankfully, I was not home-"

Walter's brow raised. "Are you in danger of..."

"Better safe than sorry, I would think in a situation like this. Hence my imminent relocation. But I'm afraid I won't feel wholly safe until the killer is caught, nor will any young woman in the city, I'd imagine. Not to mention that I do feel rather endowed with a sense of responsibility in the matter. Which is why, wise or not, I will be doing the sitting. Today."

He chewed on his thoughts for a moment before he spoke. "Of course, if your mind is made up, I will assist you."

"It is."

His glance went around the room, a flicker of sadness in his eyes. "Forgive me, I know I am prying, but I overheard the other day... I know that your parents have set certain expectations before you..." Maggie's stomach twisted. "I am worried that you will not be able to remain in the city and that our partnership will have to come to an end."

"Walter..." Maggie said, looking to offer some assurance, but there was nothing to say. She was fighting an ever ticking clock until her every freedom was stripped from her.

"I have been thinking that there may be a solution, not an ideal one, but hardly untenable, I would hope."

"What is it?"

He licked his lips and swallowed. "If what you require, to remain in the city and continue your work, which I hold in the highest esteem- If you are in need of securing an attachment, I would offer to... fill that role for you."

Maggie stared back at him as the meaning of his words washed over her. "Is that a proposal?"

"Well, I suppose it is. I understand that there is a more... romantic avenue to such things, but-"

"Oh, Walter," Maggie said, sparing him from having to continue. "I don't want to marry someone just so that I can retain my freedoms. And I couldn't do that to you. You deserve to find someone you care about, somebody worth going down *romantic avenues* for. We both do."

"I suppose I had not considered that a practical expectation for... one such as myself. For those who do not seem to conform to the *conventional tastes*..." He cleared his throat. "Pardon me, I should not have-"

"Walter, no-" Maggie said gently. What she thought she'd heard, the confession he'd half shared, was a matter of the greatest vulnerability.

He looked at her, perhaps considering if his secret would be safe in her keeping. "I supposed a partnership with a like minded person was the best I'd ever hoped for." A smile flashed weakly on his lips.

"There's hope out there for every one of us," she said, genuinely believing it.

"A comforting notion, to be sure," Walter said, removing his glasses and beginning to clean them intently. "In any case, I supposed I would offer. I would hate to see you go without knowing I had done everything I could to assist you."

Maggie stood. "Well, you could assist me in packing this place up."

"Of course," he said, joining her.

They tucked the last of her baubles and curios into the wardrobe. The books were packed away into crates. A cloth was thrown over the table to hide the *yes* and *no* carved within. A furniture cloth was found to cover her strapped chair as well. Being bolted to the floor, it was simply too much of a nuisance to move. She doubted her parents' inspection of the parlor would be thorough enough to go digging.

At last, her treasures were hidden away, the book crates stacked neatly against the wall. Her beloved parlor appeared to be nothing more than a mundane junk room of spare furniture. It stung her to see it this way. She was packing part of herself away, and fear gripped her as to whether it would ever be able to see the light again.

Maggie hardened her resolve. There was still one task she would see done. She had to keep her focus on finding Valentine.

She led the way down the stairs into the hall.

"Where are you going?" Jonathan asked as she popped into the apartment to retrieve her coat.

"I'll be going to the police station," Maggie said.

"But- You should be resting." He looked beyond her to Walter to support his case.

"I will make sure she is alright," Walter offered.

Maggie said her farewells then, even though her brother clearly would have rather protested more. She couldn't blame him for his worries, but she also could not yield to them.

CHAPTER 15

THE STREETS WERE STILL running with steady currents of water from the last night's rain, even though the sky was now a clear blue. Like the day before, the police station was utterly overrun. Walter seemed somewhat dismayed by the crowds, but Maggie pushed brazenly ahead. The desk officer scowled at her as she passed, but made no movement to stop her. Worry filled her that Harry may still be resting at home. He had mentioned working over ten hours the day before. But then, she caught a glimpse of his reddish brown hair, the cut of his shoulders through the crowd.

"Harry!" Maggie called over the hum of a dozen different conversations.

He turned at once. Catching sight of her, he tossed the files he was holding onto his desk and nodded toward a hall at the back of the room. He set a purposeful course in the same direction, and

Maggie followed, Walter at her heels. Harry led them past the holding cells into a hallway lined with mundane offices. Finally, he opened a door, revealing a staircase leading down to a basement. Maggie's breath caught in her throat as she met the chill emanating from beyond the door. This was a place of death. In the past, she had felt a similar haze hanging over churchyards, a sensation that had led to her avoiding them whenever possible.

The air only grew colder as they descended, carrying the smell of chemicals and decay. A few electric bulbs had been wired along the curved ceiling, providing an unnatural, occasionally flickering light. The opposite wall was lined with shelves bearing instruments and medical elixirs that Maggie could not name. Six metal tables were spaced along the length of the room. Only one was occupied by a figure obscured by a long, white sheet, save her face and shoulders.

"We usually use this place for mass accidents and the like until they can be identified and claimed," Harry explained as Walter took in the details of the room with unwavering interest. "She won't be here much longer. The family will come for her this afternoon."

"Good," Maggie murmured, unable to look away from the body. This was too grim and lonely a place to rest alone. As she drew nearer, Maggie's eyes settled on the features of her face. Her coloring was cool and lifeless, even her lips the dull shade of slate. Her hair was wet and limp around her. As much time as Maggie had spent among the dead, it had been in spirit alone. Yet there was something more than morbid curiosity that kept her frozen there. Maggie searched for it in poor Eileen's features until the realisation hit her. It was familiarity.

"Maggie?" Harry's voice pulled her gently from her thoughts.

"I know her," Maggie whispered. "I mean, I've seen her- I-"

"You've seen her before?" Harry asked. "Where?"

"On the day of the rally, she was there. The day we met," Maggie explained. "Someone pushed her. Camila and I helped her up- I never even knew her name, but-" But she'd been alive...

Harry's hands found her shoulders as her words failed her, steering her away. Maggie was vaguely aware as Walter came to lift the sheet over Eileen's face. Somehow, having her fully covered was more haunting than seeing her there, what was left now that her spirit was freed to that other place. ·

"You don't have to do this," Harry said, still holding her.

Maggie met his eyes, taken aback by the sincerity there. This was his best chance at finding the killer. He had all but admitted it last night, but now he was offering her a way out.

"I do," she said, and not just for his sake. If anything, she was more motivated than ever to find the man who had stolen everything from this woman, from the others as well.

Harry nodded, his touch slipping from her shoulders to his side. "So then, what now?"

She took in an icy breath. "Now we join hands."

Walter came to her side. "Will you be able to form a connection?"

Maggie nodded.

"You feel a presence lingering here?" Walter asked.

"Yes," Maggie answered. There was no singular voice in the air as there had been in the Blackbourne house or surrounding Ivy's necklace. Instead, this place carried footprints, the subtle lingering essence of many. Yet, as she reached out her senses, Maggie sensed Eileen's spirit immediately, her whispers drifting to the surface of the mist.

At last, Maggie reached out her hands. Walter's palm was familiar against her own, his steady pulse a reassurance. Yet as Harry's skin touched her own, it was another sensation entirely. At once, she could feel his heart beating throughout her whole body, twinning with her own.

A gasp loosed from her lips.

"Are you alright?" Harry asked.

Maggie nodded quickly. "Yes, quite. I will begin." She hesitated a moment and then added, "No matter what happens, do not release my hand."

She looked to Harry until he nodded in recognition. Then Maggie shut her eyes and reached. The void's frigid touch caressed her skin at once. The whisperings of a thousand voices melded together as one, their breath like frost against her ears.

"Eileen," Maggie called, reaching as she spoke. Her presence came forward obediently to her call, drifting slowly nearer. "She is with us," Maggie said, for the benefit of her companions.

She took in a deep breath and felt for the beating of her heart, of Harry's within her. Then she plunged into the Nether, reaching for Eileen's drifting presence and tying herself to it. Her breath came ragged and chilled, even as awareness of her body began to fade.

"What's happening?" Harry asked, his voice filled with concern.

"She is with me," was all Maggie said as she immersed herself in Eileen's memory.

She saw Eileen's delicate hands setting white sheets over a mattress. This scene played for her again and again, watching the cotton sheets flowing slowly down into place. It was serene, peaceful. Then she was dusting the ornate frame of a piece of art, fingers working into every crevice with care. Her hands carefully polished silverware, setting them like little soldiers in even, regimented rows. Maggie pushed past these visions.

The memories shifted to a farm in rolling hill country. A faithful dog trailed her heels as she spread feed for the chickens. She ran a brush through a horse's mane, patting its neck lovingly. Eileen was deliberately showing her these things, memories of peace and contentment.

Maggie pushed her again, sending images back. A knife. The feeling of wet brick against Katherine's back. The face of the killer. The way that Eileen's spirit struggled against these thoughts caused a tight knot of guilt to form within her. Clearly, her spirit longed for a peaceful rest… and she could have it once Maggie had seen.

The memories came to her in a violent wave as the killer's knife plunged into her gut. Maggie's knees buckled beneath her at the sudden, unexpected sensation. The vision had not even finished taking form before the pain overwhelmed her.

"Maggie!" Harry's cry sounded in her ear like a voice carried off by a distant wind.

Her lungs gasped for air as she searched the memory for every detail as it took shape around her. "I am in an alley I do not recognise," Maggie said through the tightness in her throat.

The alley was dark and very narrow. The cobblestones cradled pools of murky water that reflected the light of the streetlamps just beyond. She could feel the warmth of blood spreading over her front. The killer's arm pinned her neck against the wall. Her hands were grasping it desperately, pulling at him to make just enough room to breathe. Maggie's attention centered on him gathering every detail. It was too dark to see the features of his face as she had in Katherine's memory, but Maggie could see enough to know that it was him.

"He's wearing a black suit, like a clerk-" Maggie gasped, only to have the wind knocked from her once more by another thrust of the knife. She cried and lurched, falling as she heard a bone snap beneath the force of his blow. As her own body fell, a hand reached out and caught her waist. She struggled to breathe as her mind split between realities.

"She's in pain!" Harry protested.

"She feels the sensation of the memory," Walter explained.

Maggie gathered her courage and pushed back into the memory. She couldn't lose hold of it, or else she might miss the very thing they were looking for. The sensation of her body faded as she delved deeper. The agony was overwhelming her even as she tried to tell herself it wasn't real. Her reasoning was but a paper shield between her and the knife. Maggie tried to stay focused, to take in every detail of the scene playing before her, but what came next was nothing but a blur of pain. The knife drove into her gut again and again. Her strength was waning. All that was keeping her on her feet was the killer's hand on her throat. She had stopped fighting so long ago, but the pain would not end. Maggie could not leave Eileen to face it again alone, not when she had driven her here so harshly. Not even as the torment grew enough for her to want to shed off her skin just to be free of it.

When it finally subsided, Eileen was lying in the alley, shivering as the cold set in. There was a finality in her thoughts. Relief settled over her that it was almost over, which Maggie could not help but share as a heaviness spread through her body. Eileen's eyes shut heavily, and they both knew they would not open again.

"Stay with me," Maggie found herself saying, her own breath shaking.

The killer was doing something, and she needed to know what it was. He moved her wrists gently, setting them to pillow beneath her cheek. He brushed a hair from her brow. Then she felt his hands tickling against the back of her neck. Eileen's memory was fading. *No,* Maggie thought desperately. Then she felt it, a phantom brushing against her skin as the memory faded into oblivion.

Maggie's eyes burst open, her chest heaving suddenly. She had fallen limp into Harry's chest, who was now sitting on the floor, still holding her hand, the other arm around her waist. Walter was holding her other hand, crouched beside her uneasily. As awkward as their position was, Maggie could not make herself move.

"He stole her necklace," Maggie said, her voice hoarse and shallow through her gasping breaths. "After he moved her, he took her necklace."

Harry looked at her as if he hadn't heard her at all. He released her hand but continued to look down at her with a mystified expression. "What the livin' hell was that?"

She tried to straighten, but the memory of the pain had locked itself around her body. The fear that it would return with a single wrong motion was too great. Her brow furrowed. She had never had a companion react this way to a sitting. She wondered if the strange effect his touch held for her somehow affected him as well.

"Does she need a hospital? Her skin was cold as ice," Harry demanded of Walter. "She was hollerin' like-"

"She was experiencing Eileen's final moments," Walter explained in a pacifying tone. "The pain she experienced was only in her mind."

"Look at her!" Harry yelled. "Aren't you a doctor or something? Does she look alright to you?"

Maggie placed a hand on Harry's chest. "I'm fine," Maggie managed an even tone, even if it took extraordinary effort.

Slowly, very slowly, Maggie began to straighten, with considerable help. She could still imagine the sound of bones snapping, her lungs struggling for air. But the horrid pain did not return. Only the echoes endured.

"Maggie," Harry said as she finally found her feet, a pleading quality in his tone.

"Walter is right," Maggie said, forcing a strained smile. "It was only a memory."

Harry continued studying her, seeing through her charade, no doubt.

"You said Ms. Ward's hand was cold to the touch?" Walter said. "Would you say unnaturally so?"

He finally turned from her and swallowed. "She felt like a corpse in my hand."

Walter looked at Maggie meaningfully. "I suppose you experienced something different?" she asked.

"I would say so," Walter said. "I have often detected a drop in your temperature during times of connection, but nothing to the breadth that Officer Mulligan describes."

Maggie stored this away. They could explore later the peculiarities of Officer Mulligan when he was not before them, looking rather distressed at being discussed.

"Is it like this every time?" Harry asked. His voice was quiet, haunted.

Maggie shook her head. "I am still adjusting to such violent ends," she explained. Of course, this was an understatement. She could still feel the phantom pain in her gut, was still fighting the urge to feel if the front of her dress was indeed slick with blood.

Harry shuffled uncomfortably.

"But I saw his face. It was the same. I think he is using the same weapon as well," Maggie said, recalling every detail. "He stole Eileen's necklace, and the way he was dressed-"

"Like a clerk?" Harry said.

Maggie nodded.

"I'll see what I can make of this," he said. "I'll call on you when I know more and-"

"Actually," Maggie said, "I'm afraid I will be unavailable for a time."

Harry looked back at her, perplexed.

"After everything, I thought it wise if I relocate," she added, a terrible guilt twisting in her chest.

He only nodded, leading them up the stairs. It was a refreshing warmth to be back in the station, even amidst the dozens of people talking over one another.

"I will be seeing you again?" Harry asked just loudly enough for her to hear as she came through the door.

"Of course," Maggie said, trying to keep the smile from faltering on her face. In all honestly, she didn't know.

But even so, Maggie made herself turn, following Walter out of the station.

"You are feeling well?" Walter confirmed as they walked down the steps.

"As well as I can be," Maggie said stiffly, dropping all pretense.

Walter nodded. "I suppose that it may be some time before we see each other again."

"Yes." Maggie stopped in her tracks. "I wanted to thank you, just in case. To thank you for believing in me."

"It has been my absolute pleasure to."

"It's only- Before I met you, I'm not sure I even believed in myself," Maggie admitted with a weak laugh.

"Well, if you'll allow me, I think we've only seen the very beginnings of what you are capable of."

Maggie wrapped Walter in a tight hug, catching him thoroughly off guard, though after a beat, he returned the gesture. This couldn't be the end of everything she'd built...

But how could it not?

CHAPTER
16

MAGGIE SAT AGAINST THE SETTEE with a dismal expression. Her corset was fastened tight enough to suffocate a snake, and it wasn't even dinner. Several of her hairpins were set in so tightly it felt as if they were in danger of impaling her very skull with one wrong movement. Perhaps worst of all, her mother had insisted she be dressed in this hideously pink evening gown. Not a soft and complimentary blush or a dignified rose hue, but a flagrant shade Maggie had only before witnessed dressing saltwater taffy. On the other side of the room, her mother was sipping tea. Her back was perfectly straight as she surveyed the absolutely ridiculous pile of wedding gifts amassed at her feet. Maggie considered that she looked rather like a dragon brooding over her horde.

"Don't stare, Margaret," Mrs. Ward said, again accessing her supernatural ability to criticise Maggie without even looking at her.

Maggie let out an undignified huff and turned to watch the door instead. Her rescue would be here soon, she hoped. Camila would be coming with a gathering of her friends for her bridal shower, including her mother and two younger sisters who had just arrived in the city the night before. They would eat little cakes and open this outrageous cache of newlywed tribute as Mrs. Ward sized up her counterpart from across the aisle.

That night, there would be a family dinner, well, family and George. Her mother had been pressing her into Mr. Cromwell's company as much as possible over the past two weeks. He would talk, and Maggie would smile and try her best to convince him, and maybe even herself, that she had meant what she said about trying to open herself to the possibility of being whisked away to his English country home to become the next Lady Cromwell and breed the next little lord. Maggie rubbed her brow tiredly.

Besides her own personal troubles, she had also been avidly following the Valentine case. She would smuggle in a paper every morning while her mother was still oiling her skins, or whatever a fifty year old woman did to pretend she was still thirty something. In her mother's opinion, papers were hardly proper reading material for a lady, which it seemed was her opinion of anything worth reading.

The killer had not struck again since her relocation. Still, Maggie lived in constant dread of picking up the morning paper to find the name of another woman stamped in oversized lettering on the top of page one. Could she forgive herself if another person died while she was stuck in The Plaza like some fairytale princess in a tower? At least with her out of the apartment, Jonathan was safe. She had heard nothing from Harry or Walter, but that was hardly a surprise. Maggie was sure that prison inmates enjoyed more correspondence than she had dared. It had been her habit since childhood to hide whatever she loved from her parents with impunity, lest it be swiftly taken from her.

Finally, Camila entered, followed by her mother, who had the same generously kind aspect that Maggie remembered, even if she did look at her wit's end with her two younger daughters. Mrs. Ward offered nothing more than a cold, imperious stare as they settled politely onto the settee.

Mrs. Huddleston cleared her throat mildly. "It was so good of you to invite us, Mrs. Ward," she commented, her tone guarded by an iron wall of courtesy. "It is a pleasure to meet you in person before the day is upon us. Though I've heard so much."

Camila had warned her then, Maggie thought, smirking into her teacup.

"Well, I'm sure someone had to host a meeting between our families before the wedding," Mrs. Ward said, adding tartly, "Normally, such things are hosted by the bride's family, but our accommodations are certainly more suitable for such a thing. Don't think it's any trouble at all though. I do enjoy hosting, and Heaven knows my daughter has not required her mother for such things, though I hope soon enough."

And with that, her mother had managed to offend every individual in the room without even setting down her tea. The older of the two girls looked up at her mother in utter astonishment. Maggie envied her greatly in that moment that such cruelty was a stranger to her.

"Well, you have our thanks," Mrs. Huddleston said with a clearly false smile, "and this tea is excellent."

From there, the afternoon carried on more gracefully. Camila's friends arrived. Maggie recognised many of them from suffrage events. One even wore a ribbon of purple and gold on her chest, to which Maggie heard her mother hiss at the poor girl that this was afternoon tea, not a political rally. Camila had swooped in then quite heroically to divert her. This incident aside, having established herself, Maggie's mother was happier to sit in quiet judgement, making only the occasional wicked comment.

The centerpiece of the afternoon was Camila's opening of the gifts, which took a good deal of time, as there were many. Yet somehow, she seemed equally delighted by every one. When the affair had reached its conclusion, two of the hotel valets came to clean the wrappings as the ladies broke apart to discuss the impending nuptials.

"Ms. Ward," one of the valets came to Maggie's side. It was a casual exchange, but something made her hair stand on end, like a cold wind on the back of her neck. She turned rather flustered to see the young valet holding something out to her. "Sorry to startle you, miss," he said, holding out a small wrapped box. "This was discarded in the papers."

Maggie looked at the little present for a moment, listening to its icy whispers. She had to remind herself to lift her hand to accept it. "Thank you," she tried to say casually, but likely failed. In any case, he nodded and moved on.

Her eyes went back to the package in her palm. Its cool embrace tickled against her skin as her heart beat faster in her chest. It was unaddressed, wrapped in simple parchment paper, tied with a string, which was odd, as so many of the gifts had been wrapped as extravagantly as possible. But curiouser by far, what caused Maggie's hand to tremble, it was laced with death. A spirit was hovering over this gift. Maggie's mind raced as she scanned the crowd for Camila. She was talking with a pair of friends who Maggie recognised, but could not name.

"Camila," Maggie said, struggling to hold a smile on her cheeks. "So sorry to steal her away," she said, turning to her companions.

"What is it?" Camila asked, stepping away. "Are you alright? I know your mother has been-"

"It's not that." Maggie brushed the idea aside quickly. "I've found a gift that got lost in the jumble, and it doesn't have a name." She tried to keep her composure casual and fared better than she had expected. Camila picked it up, completely unfazed by the bone chilling mist that Maggie could not ignore.

"You know, I do remember this one," Camila said. "It was left at my apartment. Most of them have been sent to my parents or yours, but this one must have been posted to me directly. The return address said it was one of my father's employees- Goodness, his name, I've utterly forgotten. I feel horrible, and it was so kind of him to send a gift."

Maggie began to fidget, unable to help herself as nerves crawled over her skin. "What's inside?" She was being a terrible coward, but she needed to know and couldn't risk touching the thing herself, not here, not after what happened with Ivy's necklace.

Camila tore the paper and revealed a worn velvet box. Inside was a shining locket on a golden chain. Maggie stumbled a step back, heart hammering.

"Oh, it's lovely," Camila said, running her finger over the chain. "I must remember so I can-" Her face lit with recognition. "Howard! That was it. Howard Towlson."

Nausea twisted violently in her gut.

She was well and truly going to lose her stomach right here on the floor. That necklace that whispered of the void... There was no doubt in her mind that if she touched it, she would see the visions of Eileen's blood spreading over the alleyway. Maggie could almost feel the sensation of the killer slipping the necklace over her skin as her final memory faded.

Karina had recognised her sketch as *Howard*.

Howard Towlson. His name beat through her body.

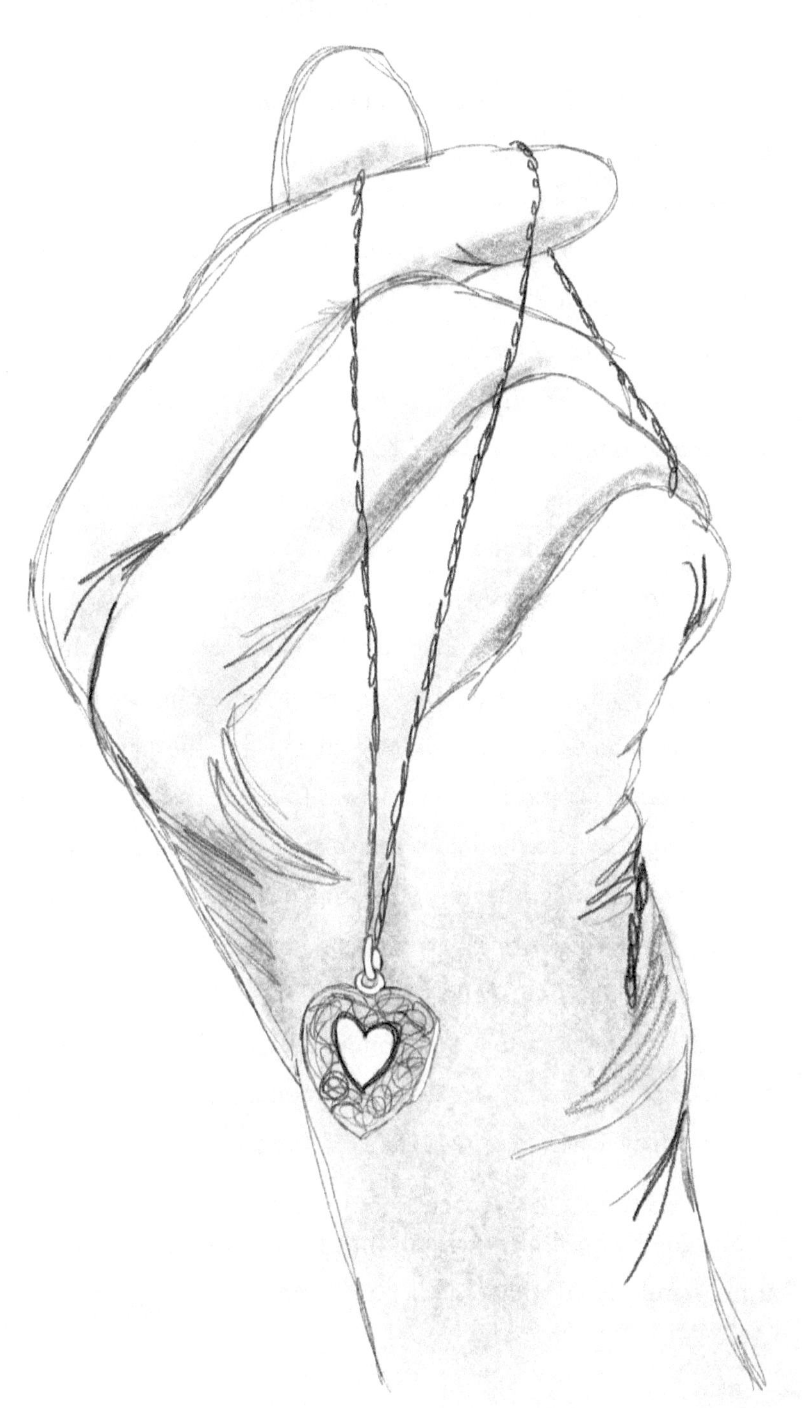

Could it be this simple, to stumble onto his identity by chance?

How could it not be him?

"I have to go," Maggie said, unsure if Camila heard her, as she set a straight course to the door.

"Margaret," her mother's voice stopped her in her tracks.

She turned reluctantly, her mind too anxious to formulate any kind of excuse as to why she would leave the suite.

"Go down to the lobby and ask them what champagne they are serving at tonight's dinner," she said.

"Of course," Maggie said breathlessly.

She endured several torturous moments of her mother complaining about the substandard nature of American valets and recalling every bottle of disappointing champagne she'd ever had the misfortune of tasting, but then she was free.

The trip down to the lobby passed in a blur as Maggie was occupied by her own thoughts. Howard Towlson. Watchie. The Valentine Ripper. Eileen's killer, who had stolen her necklace... and mailed it to Camila as a gift?

The elevator stopped at the ground floor, and Maggie's focus fixed on the concierge. She crossed the lobby at once.

"How may I help you, Ms. Ward?" the well dressed young man asked.

Maggie silenced her nervous heart and offered her most charming smile, laced with a subtle hint of mischief.

His brows raised, and he leaned in ever so slightly. That caught his attention then. Good.

"I have a rather strange request," Maggie said, voice low and leading. "One that requires… discretion."

"How may I help you, Ms. Ward?" his voice dropped its formal air and lowered to a conspiratorial murmur.

"I will require some stationary," she began, "and the delivery of a message, a very private message."

He retrieved the paper without delay and laid it out before her.

"Of course," he said. "The Plaza holds its guests' privacy in paramount respect."

Maggie smiled, looking through her lashes, before she quickly penned the only words necessary. *Howard Towlson is Valentine. Associated with Huddleston Textiles. -Maggie.* Pleased, she enclosed the message in an envelope and wrote on the exterior the correct address for one Officer Harry Mulligan, NYPD.

She slid the paper over the countertop. The concierge's eyes widened slightly as he saw the address. Scandalous, to say the least, mysterious, likely enough to run the rumor mill in this place for the next year. So be it, Maggie thought, as long as her mother never heard a breath of it.

"Thank you," Maggie said, casting her eyes at the name stitched into his uniform, "Timothy." Risking being rather obvious, Maggie shot him a final coquettish look before departing. It was a ridiculous notion, Maggie thought to herself as she walked away. When flirting with most young men, there was no such thing as too obvious.

It wasn't until she was back upstairs, alone in the hallway, that Maggie let out her held breath. Yet still, the tension would not release its grip on her thoughts. She finally had a name. Harry would have it soon. But would it be enough?

Her worries did not leave her, not for a single moment through the afternoon, even as they sat through dinner. Thankfully, the entire party was focused on Jonathan and Camila as they navigated all her mother's sour comments that Camila had stuck to her decision to use her church instead of The Plaza for the ceremony. As always, George was happy to carry the conversation, which Maggie was very grateful for tonight. No one noticed that she hardly spoke a word.

After dinner, they broke out to the parlor for brandies. Jonathan and Camila were locked in conversation with their parents. Maggie didn't envy them in the slightest. But in her observation, they were holding their own quite well against her parents' endless assaults to overtake the wedding to their vision, even at this late hour.

George came to her side with a cocktail in hand. Maggie took it perhaps too eagerly. Anything to calm her nerves. Was the killer already in hand? Had her message somehow gotten lost before reaching its destination? How would she even know? Having to wait for word until the morning papers came seemed like torture. There'd be no sleep for her tonight.

She took a long drink.

"They seem very happy," George mused.

Maggie followed his gaze stupidly. Obviously, he was talking about Jonathan and Camila. "Yes, as different as they are, they are suited well for one another," Maggie commented.

"I rather agree," George said, looking back at her. "Often it is differing personalities that draw two people together, complement each other."

It was evident in his gaze he was no longer speaking about the bride and groom to be. Maggie drank again, acknowledging herself for the coward she was.

George turned his body, blocking the others from her view and looking at her intently. "I thought we had agreed to try," he murmured.

"We did," Maggie confessed, "and George, you have been rather wonderful company these past weeks. My mind is just far from me tonight."

"It often seems far away," George commented quietly.

Maggie looked back at him, unsure of what to say.

"Mine is often with my home," George said, looking rather wistful. "Is it the same for you? Do your thoughts drift to what you are passionate about?"

Maggie let out a small chuckle. Her mind had been hovering over the outcome of a morbid police investigation for weeks on end. Was that what she was passionate about? "I suppose so," Maggie said.

"Tell me then," he pressed. "What are your passions?"

Maggie stumbled a moment, startled by the personal nature of his question, the intent look in his eyes. "Helping people, I suppose. People who are grieving… or have been hurt."

He processed her response for several moments. "A noble answer… and not what I would have expected."

"What should I have said? My needlework and the pianoforte?" Maggie scoffed. "It's a new age, George. There's more to a woman, to a person, than handicrafts, and-" she stopped herself. The brandy had officially gotten away from her.

To her surprise, George's shoulders shook in stifled laughter. "I have always known there was more to you than handicrafts."

Maggie's cheeks flushed. He was being charming, utterly charming… and then her heart twisted painfully in her chest. The image of a dark haired man huddled in a muddy trench somewhere in France flashed through her mind. She shivered. Something deep inside her felt as though it was weeping, or bleeding. She could never tell which.

George's brow furrowed, confused by her sudden change. He was about to speak when his gaze lifted. Maggie followed it, sitting straight the moment she saw Timothy, the concierge, approaching them.

"There's a gentleman in the lobby for you, Ms. Ward," he whispered to her discreetly.

She stood at once, all other thoughts forgotten. "Of course," Maggie said, turning to George. "Please excuse me. I'll only be a moment."

Maggie did everything in her power not to look as if she were crawling out of her skin as she left the suite parlor. She sweetly told the elevator valet to take her down to the lobby. Even at this moment, she knew her parents' minds would be churning with scandalous theories as to who on earth could have called her away from their dinner party. As far as they were concerned, every person of import in her life was already upstairs. Thankfully, convention would keep them up there as Maggie worked frantically on a story that they might believe. Having been called by mistake was a last resort they would never swallow.

A sigh of relief escaped her as the elevator doors opened to the lobby. Maggie set out at a pace verging on urgency. Harry was waiting there, his uniform unbuttoned at the top, telling her he was no longer on duty. His shoulders were high and tense in agitation. Her steps slowed. Why was he upset? Was another girl dead? Did the killer slip through his fingers even though she'd given him everything? Had she been... wrong?

As he caught sight of her, his eyes widened in acknowledgement, but then something more. His look was so searching, Maggie couldn't help but follow his gaze. She supposed he had never seen her dressed in evening wear. Even if she detested the saccharine color, it was far finer than her casual dress. But he didn't seem charmed by her appearance. If anything, it seemed to upset him more. It was such a startling response that she stopped in her tracks. Harry closed the distance.

"What is this?" he said, holding something tight in his fist. She realised a second later that it was her letter.

"I have his name," Maggie said, still rather disarmed by his aggressive tone. "I sent it to you as soon as I could. I was hoping you could find an address, perhaps."

"Is this a game to you?" His voice was tense and barely below a whisper.

"Of course not!" Maggie shot back, dismayed.

"Haven't seen you for two weeks. You said you were going away for your safety, and I understood. But this? This is where you've been?" He gestured to the grand hotel around them.

Maggie shook her head. "Harry, no. It's not like that!" For Heaven's sake, she was starting to tear up. Here he was, thinking she had abandoned him for some swell holiday. How could she make him understand that the last weeks had been utter torture?

"Been workin' ten hour days at the station. I barely sleep for working on this. And you beg me to let you help, only to disappear into this?"

"I'm doing everything I can. I promise."

"Is that right?" he gestured to her, clearly still angry, but listening.

Maggie was still searching for the words to even begin to describe that her life was currently in a state of well mannered cataclysm when another voice called to her from the direction of the elevators. She clenched her eyes shut tight. This couldn't be happening.

"Margaret?" George called to her again. He came to her side, perfectly polished in his white tie.

Harry looked from her to him mutinously.

"Is there an issue I can assist you with, Officer?" George asked, noting with disapproval his untidy appearance and agitated state.

Harry's eyes locked with hers. "What is this, Maggie?"

She could scream, right here in this lobby, but no, the shrill sound remained trapped within her skull. This couldn't be happening. To admit the nature of her association with Harry in front of George was suicide. He'd have so many questions. Her carefully balanced game would crash around her. Yet she could already see the pain beneath Harry's anger. She couldn't abandon him, push him aside as if he were a stranger.

"Officer Mulligan." Maggie picked each word with deadly precision. "This is my dear friend, Mr. George Cromwell." She turned to George with a carefree expression. "I'm so sorry I was called away. Officer Mulligan has been generously assisting me with a matter in his free time. He had news to share with me rather urgently."

She fell quiet, praying that Harry would understand why she had not shared details of their partnership and that George would have the decency not to ask.

"I will let you get back to your dinner," Harry said. His expression was hardened, impossible to read.

"You will think about what I said?" Maggie called after him as desperation gripped her.

He only nodded once before stepping heavily toward the doors. It took everything in her to keep her eyes from budding with tears. Maggie wanted nothing more than to follow him, to make sure he was alright...to make sure he was going to follow through with the name she had found. But she had already exposed herself too much. Her knees felt weak as George offered his arm.

Maggie laced her arm in his and followed absently as he led her back toward the elevator. She said nothing as they were carried up to the proper floor. In fact, Maggie didn't find her voice until the doors closed behind them, depositing them in the hall. Whatever she had decided to say was promptly forgotten as George said the unimaginable.

"You do not need to worry yourself," he murmured. "I will say nothing to your parents."

Maggie swallowed her shock.

George sighed. "Though I must ask if I should be concerned about your relationship with the officer..."

"My- My relationship- Oh goodness, George, no. It's not like that at all."

He nodded, seeming a measure reassured.

Maggie bit her lip. She was giving him hope where there was none. She knew that. Harry may have no hold over her heart, but it was still a far thing from free and willing. As they returned to the parlor, dread settled in her stomach. This careful game she was playing would not survive much longer, and when it fell to pieces, it would not be without its casualties. That truth settled heavily on her, the dreadful realisation that when this came apart, as she knew it must, she would not be the only one to get hurt.

CHAPTER
17

HARRY KNOCKED BACK ANOTHER whiskey, letting the glass come down forcefully on the bar top. Rolling his lips, he uncrumpled the paper at his side. The letter was worn and wrinkled from being repeatedly balled up and smoothed out again. Still, he could make out Maggie's neat script and his own below it. Before he had even gone to The Plaza, he had found the address for Howard Towlson. It stared at him now, taunting him. He could have the answer here in his hand, yet he was bloody miserable. *Could...* it all came down to that word. This could be the answer, or she *could* be leading him in circles.

There was nothing to suggest that this Howard Towlson was the killer, other than her own word. Harry had looked into the man: no criminal record at all. A clerk at the textile factory, Maggie had mentioned. What if she just had a vendetta against this man, and this was all some complex way of framing him? Harry sighed as yet another insane theory circled his mind. He'd been at it so long, sitting on this wobbly barstool at Mullarkey's Pub, that they all seemed possible now.

What he'd seen in the morgue had been something for sure. He still had nightmares, hearing her call out like that, holding her ice cold against his chest. Sometimes, it was just comforting to think that she had just been acting, but that never sat right. Who would act out *that*? It was insane to think she would go through all this just to frame a man, but the alternative... Well, that was crazy too.

Maggie was an enigma. Every time he thought he had a hold of who she was, she showed him some new angle. She was like smoke slipping through his fingers. Harry liked to think he understood people pretty well. Especially since he joined the force, he had learned how to read people fast working the streets. But even now, he couldn't seem to hold her down.

There was the Maggie he'd found in the alley, fearless and determined, a ball of fire in a dress. The same one who'd insisted that Ivy was involved in the Valentine case no matter what he had to say. Then there was the Maggie who'd sat at that bar table over there. The one who threw back whiskey and beers as they talked about the case, the one who'd danced through the night with him. Once she'd gotten her head out of her worries, once she started to smile... He hadn't been able to look away.

Of course, he'd seen another side of her in that morgue, one he would never forget as long as he lived. She had been so focused, centered, and if that had really been true, god damn tenacious. But then tonight at the Plaza... Seeing her in that dress, all done up, with that swell on her arm. She didn't look like herself at all, at least not the woman he thought he knew. The more he thought about it, the more he saw how broken she'd looked under all that polish. All he could think was, how could all those people live together in one body?

Pat came by with a sympathetic look that he met with a grimace. At least the bartender refilled his glass.

"You should get home to yer poor mam," Pat said.

"Not tonight, Pat," Harry said, taking a sip.

He huffed. "Your uptown girl's got ya all tied in a knot, eh?"

His lips twisted sourly again. "She's not my girl, Pat."

Pat just shrugged, looking amused, but moved on. Harry could wring the man's neck if he wasn't like an uncle to him.

Harry rubbed his face. It was getting very late, and he was exhausted, but he had made some sort of wordless vow not to leave this stool without a decision. If he went after Howard and he wasn't the killer, it could ruin his career. Hell, it wasn't even his case, and he'd already been crossing lines in his work with Maggie. He'd always been impulsive, but this... He blew out a breath and emptied his glass. Then again, a small voice in his mind whispered to him, what if? What if Maggie was everything she claimed to be? What if he actually held the killer's name in his hand? What if he sat on this and another woman died?

In the end, that was what made up his mind. Could he trust Maggie? He had no idea. God, he wanted to, a small and not altogether sober voice within him rang. But either way, he'd never been one to do nothing.

By morning, Harry's resolution had formed into a plan. It was still early when he walked up the path of narrow brownstones until he came to number 780. His was the first floor apartment, registered under his mother, Gail Towlson. In the window, the drapes were drawn, obscuring any view within. Below them, an assortment of flowers were in healthy bloom. It hardly looked like the lair of a killer. Perhaps Howard no longer lived here? Perhaps Howard was entirely innocent...

Harry pushed the thought away and walked up the steps. It was early into the workday. With any luck, Mr. Towlson would be at the textile factory, and his mother would be obliging. He pulled back the polished knocker.

There was movement on the other side of the door, faint sounds. Every second that passed crawled over his skin. Was he escaping out the back? Destroying evidence? Harry forced a deep breath through his nose. Mr. Towlson had no reason to be suspicious. He probably wasn't even here.

It was the elderly Mrs. Towlson who answered the door, opening it only a crack. She was a tiny woman, hunched with age.

"Is everything alright, officer? Is my Howard well? He hasn't been in any sort of accident, has he?" she asked very quickly.

"No, ma'am," he said gently. "I'm sure your son is just fine. We think he may have been a witness to a crime in your neighborhood."

"He's not here," Mrs. Towlson fretted.

"Can I ask you some questions, Mrs. Towlson?"

"Of course," she smiled and opened the door wider.

Harry ducked inside and followed her through to a small sitting room. At once, the sour smell of decay filled his nose. The interior was cluttered beyond his previous imagination. The piano in the corner was buried under rotting papers. Teacups had been forgotten on nearly every surface of the room, many of them half filled and now layered with mold. Mrs. Towlson seemed upset by the clutter, as if she was only just realising the state of things. She began to mutter apologies, fluttering about the room, picking up items only to set them back down in another space.

"Mrs. Towlson, it's alright, ma'am," Harry said, trying to calm her. It twisted his heart to see the poor woman living in this filth. How could a son let his mother live this way? "Thank you kindly for welcomin' me into your home."

Mrs. Towlson smiled in a dazed sort of fashion that told him plainly enough what he'd already wondered. This woman was no longer in possession of her full mind.

"Well, have a seat," she said, looking between the two armchairs. One was piled high with senseless clutter, topped of course with a teacup. The other was sunken from use and carried a very foul smell.

Harry raced forward before she could trouble herself and emptied the other chair. Before he had finished, she had already settled herself in the sunken chair. Another stab of pity pierced through him. Then something else caught his eye. The mantlepiece was one orderly facet among the utter chaos. The only surface that was totally bare except for a row of carefully maintained picture frames. It was not even plagued by the thick layer of dust that blanketed the rest of the room. Yet if he was any judge, Mrs. Towlson's small frame would be too short to dust along the high surface.

"These are lovely pictures," Harry said absently to offer an excuse as he inspected them further.

Her expression brightened with recognition. "That at the end is my dear Ed. There's my Howard as a boy and just some years ago." Harry's eyes stopped on the picture of adult Howard. It was a damn near perfect match to the sketch Maggie had given him.

He held back a shiver. It didn't mean anything. If she had chosen Howard at the beginning of her charade, of course, all her evidence would point to him. Beside his picture was a smaller photo in a much finer frame. Perhaps it was even gold plated, Harry thought as he looked closer. It certainly seemed out of place among the others.

"Who did you say this was?" Harry asked. She was beautiful, with dark curls and sharp eyes. In her portrait, she was dressed expensively.

"Oh, that's Howard's fiancée," Mrs. Towlson said wistfully, "Camila."

The significance of her words circled him for a moment before he was able to grasp it. Camila was the name of Maggie's companion, who had been arrested along with her the day they'd met. The one who had been bailed by her fiancé, Maggie's brother… certainly not Howard Towlson.

"Have you met Camila?" he asked, still unsure. Their meeting had been weeks ago. Perhaps he was mistaken.

Mrs. Towlson shuffled. "I will soon, Howard says. But I need to clean the apartment first." Her expression became further troubled. "He can't have her over in this filth."

Something in the way she spoke suggested those words were not her own. The sick pit in his stomach twisted again.

"I think you just need a little help, yeah?" Harry said. He couldn't bear seeing her this upset. "You have a very lovely home. Sometimes, we all just need a little help."

Mrs. Towlson took a deep breath. That dazed expression filtered into her eyes again. "Would you like some tea?"

Harry bit his cheek punishingly, as what he had to do was clear before him. He hated that it felt as though he was using the old woman, but it was ultimately for her own good. "D'you know where Howard keeps his records, Mrs. Towlson?"

"His office is just down the hall," she said, a worried expression cast over her features. "He doesn't like me to go back there. I just mess everything."

Harry sighed. Whether or not this Howard was a killer, Harry was about ready to beat some decency into him. "I'll do my best to leave everything as it was, shall I? And you can make us some tea."

Mrs. Towlson nodded finally. "I'll put the kettle on." It was a struggle for her to get to her feet, but Harry followed her patiently as she shuffled out of the sitting room. The dining room beyond was buried in a hoard of filthy clutter. The kitchen, however, was the source of the rotten smell: spoiled food. It clung to plates and pots piled over the counters precariously. There was likely not a clean dish in the entire room.

Rage coursed through him as she moved about it, as if nothing were amiss. If a man could reduce his mother to this, he was capable of anything. Harry forced himself to focus. Resolve was settling itself heavily in his mind. He tried the first door down the hall. He'd been invited inside the house by the tenant, Harry reminded himself. This was perfectly legal. If he found anything, he'd be back within the hour with a team to collect it into evidence.

The office was immaculate. He had expected as much, but still, he was filled with bitter disgust. It was a minimal space with a rolltop desk and a bookshelf. Just above the desk was a hand drawn rendering of the same woman, Camila.

Harry did not hesitate to open the desk. The top was scattered with clerks' ledgers and mundane papers. He sifted through them, heart hammering. A sense of finality was closing in on him. This was it, the precipice. There was a leather bound journal which he opened and yielded nothing more than financial accounts.

With frustration, Harry slid open the first drawer. It was nothing but common office supplies. Then the next. More leather journals stacked one on top of another. Harry growled and slammed it shut. He scanned the titles on the bookshelves, but they were of no importance. The floorboards creaked as he paced the room. The sound prompted him to check for perhaps a loose board, a hidden hiding place.

The blood was pulsing in his ears as he finally stood with nothing. Back to the desk. He ruffled through the papers again, rummaged through the drawer of supplies. He picked up one of the journals. A strand of human hair traced over his fingers. His skin pricked as if from the cold.

Harry tore open the journal. These weren't ledgers, but pages and pages of hand scrawled penciling. Details of a woman's movements. Times, streets, physical descriptions, associations. He turned the pages feverishly until a hand sketched portrait of Eileen stared back at him. The feeling left his hands, the journal nearly slipping from his fingers.

He slammed the journal down on the desk and picked up the next: Mary Foster. The next: Katherine Read. Each of them contained a lock of hair. Harry's hands were shaking. A cold sweat had formed on his back, his brow. There were four more journals.

Four more dead girls? He could only think of one. He picked them all up. None of these contained hair. Maybe that meant…

Harry opened the first. Camila. The contents were different. There were descriptions of her movements, as there had been with the others, but there were also love letters, imagined scenarios. Mrs. Towlson's words came to him. Camila was his fiancée, or so he said. He looked at the bottom most journal. The dates began two years ago. Christ Almighty. Harry blew out a breath.

The shriek of the kettle nearly made him jump out of his skin. Harry put everything as it was in a feverish rush. This was it. Howard killed those girls. If they looked further, they would only find more evidence of it, he was sure.

That meant that Maggie had been right, completely terrifyingly right.

CHAPTER

18

MAGGIE WOKE TO THE BLESSED SIGHT of her own bedroom on Warren Street. This was it: her last day of freedom. She lay in bed a moment longer, contemplating the surreal notion. Her mother would be well occupied with Jonathan and Camila for the entire day. The wedding was only four days away now. This would be the last of them where Maggie would not be wholly possessed by the preparations. She'd made enough excuses the evening before to stay one final night at the apartment. Perhaps it was a foolish thing to do, but she couldn't deny herself the last chance to sleep in her own bed.

Maggie contemplated the possibilities of how she might spend these precious hours. Her parlor was already packed away, her brother and Camila gone for the day. She supposed a walk in Central Park would be nice, and of course, visiting Walter. This would be her last chance... and that pub Harry had taken her to. She wanted to drink beer and dance again. Harry probably wouldn't go with her though. She hadn't heard a thing from him since he left The Plaza, two days ago now. He'd probably discounted the name she had given him. Maggie sat up in bed grumpily. That's what she wanted the most, to know that Valentine was off the streets. That he was locked up in a dark hole somewhere where he'd never hurt anyone ever again.

A growl of frustration escaped her as Maggie threw off the covers. All the hazy serenity she had felt upon waking had dissipated under the heat of purposeful focus. She was going to go to the station. If Harry wouldn't listen, maybe someone else would. They couldn't all discount her. At least one would look into what she said, right?

She was dressed earlier than usual and found herself in the odd position of having a fresh, hot breakfast. Mrs. Doyle noted her early rise with no small amount of suspicion but kept her mouth thankfully shut about it. Jonathan had stayed the night at the Plaza, so it was a strangely quiet morning. Maggie was just polishing off her tea when the door sounded.

Mrs. Doyle brushed past, muttering something about *all hours* and *manners*. Maggie found herself smiling ruefully into her cup. She really was going to miss everything about this place, even Mrs. Doyle and her fussing.

"Oh, good morning, officer." Her voice sounded high with surprise, drawing Maggie's attention at once. "Please, come inside."

Maggie let out a low stream of indecent speech as she hurried from the table. She came casually striding into the sitting room just as Harry removed his hat. For once, he was not wearing his policeman's uniform. Instead, he wore a loose fitting wool suit over a collarless shirt. Clearly, it had not been tailored to his frame and had endured its share of wear. Mrs. Doyle gave Maggie a lingering glance before she left them to attend to the breakfast dishes.

When they were alone, words crowded her mind, questions, greetings, apologies, until she found herself in the mortifying position of saying absolutely nothing at all.

"Ms. Ward," he greeted her formally, combing a hand back through his auburn hair.

That couldn't possibly be a good sign, could it? "Officer Mulligan," she responded in kind.

His lips stiffened slightly, but he continued on. "You were right," he said quietly.

"What?" She felt as though her knees would give way beneath her, but at the same time, she could not move.

"Howard Towlson is the Valentine Ripper," he said, tone solemn.

"You caught him?" Maggie asked breathlessly.

Harry's gaze lowered, and he shook his head. "Don't have him in custody, but we are watching his house. Every officer in the city has been lookin' for him since last night."

Maggie swallowed, moving to the settee to sit. Harry followed, perching on the edge of Jonathan's armchair.

"How did you know it was him?" she asked, one of a hundred questions blustering about her mind. "To be honest, I didn't think you believed me after the other night."

He pushed his hand through his hair again and sighed. "I owe ya an apology, Maggie. *Honestly,* I didn't know what to think that night... but it didn't make it right the way I treated you. I didn't know if I could trust you or not. I still don't understand you, Maggie. Like I said before, you don't make a lick of sense, but that's no excuse… In the end, I couldn't forgive myself if you were right, and I didn't do a thing about it."

"And I was?" Maggie could barely breathe.

Harry traced his lips with his fingers. "There were journals in his home, detailin' the movements of the women he killed… Found drafts of the letter he left with Eileen's body. The handwriting was a match." His words were slow and careful. Maggie got the sense there was something more.

"He hasn't killed anyone else, has he?" Maggie asked.

Harry shook his head with a heaviness that suggested there *was* something else. Something bad. He pulled a paper from his pocket, a hand drawn sketch. "D'you know this woman?"

Maggie took the picture. Her brows narrowed. The woman in the sketch, her dark brows and full lips, sharp eyes and almond shaped face. It was clearly Camila. "What is this?" she choked out the words.

"I found that in his apartment," Harry said.

"He gave Camila the necklace that he stole from Eileen. That's how I knew…" Maggie whispered. Her mind found that train of thought it had abandoned that night. She'd been too distracted by everything to find it again...

Harry nodded heavily. "He had four journals filled with notes about her movements, going back two years."

"What?" she managed, as the air was stolen from her lungs.

"He's been following her. His mother was under the impression that they were courtin' for some time. I think he built an affair between them in his mind. In his room, we found a box of possibly stolen personal effects, newspaper clippings of her engagement." His eyes flicked to the ground for a second before he carried on. "I looked into the dates. Ivy was killed the day after the engagement announcement between Ms. Huddleston and your brother first appeared in the paper."

Maggie shook her head.

"Eileen was killed the same day the paper posted the time and place of the ceremony."

"No," Maggie said, standing. Her hand came to cover her mouth. Pieces were fitting together in her mind, creating a conclusion she refused to acknowledge. "This can't be right!"

Harry stood beside her, his demeanor trying to extend some manufactured calm to her as well. "I believe the knife in your door was an act of aggression against your brother, not you."

"That's insane!" Maggie shouted, surprising even herself. "You can't think that! You're wrong. Why would anyone want to hurt Jonathan?"

"Has there been anythin' else? Has he been followed? Suspicious letters?"

Maggie shook her head again, clinging to her denial. But it was fitting together too perfectly to ignore. "His window- His office window was broken weeks ago… They never- Oh, God." Maggie fell back into the settee, feeling suddenly heavy. "It was the day after Mary Foster was killed," she murmured.

"Breathe, Maggie," Harry said steadily as he crouched before her until their eyes were level.

"They're getting married in four days!" Maggie choked as her chest tightened.

"We'll do everything we can," Harry said. "He won't touch them. Hey, look at me now."

Maggie forced her frantic eyes to still as his hand settled on her arm.

"Breathe now," he said evenly.

Maggie did, uneasily at first.

"I think they are both in danger," he explained. "Towlson's obsessed with her. That much is obvious. I think it was her engagement that caused him to begin killing. I think-"

"No!" Maggie growled. "It is not Camila's fault he killed those women. He made his own choices."

Harry nodded in agreement. "You're right. It isn't her fault. I only mean that it was his anger at her for getting engaged to someone else that led him to kill the others. Ivy was unplanned, an outburst of rage. I looked into things yesterday, and Katherine was a close associate of Camila's."

Maggie nodded. "I did a sitting with her roommate, Laura. Camila introduced us. They all went to church together. She knew Mary socially as well, but not closely. And Eileen, they only met once for a moment…" Cool dread coated her skin. "He was watching, wasn't he?"

He lowered his eyes. The sickness only grew, building in her throat. How many times had he been watching, and they never knew? Had he killed all those girls just because they'd been misfortunate enough to get too close to the woman he was really angry with? "Do you think- Was he trying to punish her?"

Harry gave a weighty sigh. "I think he took out his frustrations as close to Camila as he could. Katherine was killed on Valentine's Day. We always thought that was where he came up with the *leaving a Valentine* idea. Mary was engaged, just like her. I think, in some sick way, he's got love and rage all mixed into one. He kills because he's angry, because he loves her, and he's all but invisible to her."

Maggie grimaced as the sickness churned in her stomach. "It's no excuse."

"You're right." Harry caught her gaze and nodded until Maggie knew in her bones that he understood. There was no explanation that would shift the blame from this man's shoulders. No excuse for killing innocent people, no matter how much pain he was in.

His fingers trailed his lips before he carried on. "You said that your brother's office window was busted the day after Mary's murder?"

"He found it the next day," Maggie explained. "It might have been broken the day before, the day of the murder, I mean. I only remember because it was right before- before the engagement party."

Harry nodded thoughtfully. "Then Eileen was killed when the announcement of the ceremony came out in the paper. He leaves the knife in your door…"

"It was a threat for Jonathan," Maggie agreed. "I thought it was for me…" Her voice trailed off, leaving only heavy silence.

"What now?" Maggie said finally, perhaps a little too forcefully. "Clearly, he's lashed out with every mention of the wedding. What's he going to do on the actual day? It's only four days away!"

Harry's sharp blue eyes centered on her own. His voice began steady and assured. "He knows we're looking. That's why he hasn't been home. He knows it's only a matter of time until we catch him. So… I think he's gonna do one of two things."

Maggie gestured anxiously for him to go on.

Harry sighed. "He's either gonna run, like the Captain says. Most of the force thinks he's gonna try to leave the city. They're covering the stations and the ports." He shook his head. "But I think he might go after her, Camila."

Hollow fear raged through her veins. "Why?" The word was quiet and open, asking a hundred questions all at once. Harry only answered one.

Harry blew out a breath. "He loves her. He hates her. He's out of his mind, but from what I saw, everything he's done, it's been about her. He's not a common crook who's going to skip town to avoid the heat. He's obsessed. I think he'll see this through to the end."

"We've got to do something, and she can't know," Maggie said, standing again suddenly and beginning to pace. "Jonathan either, not ever. They're getting married! And they are so happy. They deserve to be happy."

"They're in danger," he insisted.

"I can't." There had to be a way, a way that kept them safe without ruining everything.

"So, what do you think we should do? Let 'em wander the city blindly?"

"They won't be wandering the city. They'll be at The Plaza, except for a few appointments."

Harry nodded, his mind clearly working as well. "What about the wedding?"

"What about it? There will be hundreds of people there," Maggie said. "He's hardly going to run up the aisle and-" A cool sweat covered her skin. Maggie tried to steady herself, resisting the urge to vomit at the thought of Camila's blood spilling over her white dress.

"The entire day?" Harry questioned. "He knows the time and the place of the wedding. It would only make sense that he'd be there or as close as he could get."

Maggie chewed her lip.

Harry's hands settled on his hips. "A crowd like that might even be the perfect way for him to get close to her."

She dropped down on the settee, holding her head in her hands. "This can't be happening." She was the one who invited danger into her life. She was the one who took risks. Jonathan and Camila just wanted to get married, to start a family, a life together.

"We'll keep them safe," he whispered, his voice soft like a promise.

Maggie sniffed, wiping her eyes. Honestly, what was crying going to help? "Come to the wedding," she said firmly, looking up at him.

"What?"

"If he's still… loose by the wedding, I want you to come. You can keep them safe, and they don't have to know. You'll just be there as my friend."

Harry watched her, weighing the idea.

"Do you have a white tie?" Maggie asked, again looking over his ill fitting suit.

Finally, he nodded. "It's a good idea, and yeah, I'll manage something, if your people will go for it."

"My people?" Maggie questioned before his meaning settled on her. "Oh, they'll hate it," she gave a small laugh. "But what are they going to do about it? They're already taking everything from me."

His brows narrowed. "What d'you mean?"

Maggie blanched as she realised what she'd said.

Harry settled back into the armchair, sitting on the very edge, elbows resting on his legs. "What's going on, Maggie?"

She hesitated, ashamed. It all seemed so insignificant in light of everything else. "My parents... They told me some time ago that if I wasn't engaged by my brother's wedding, I'd have to move back home with them."

Harry looked at her, not as though her situation was petty, but as though he knew there was more to it than just that. He waited.

"I'll lose my business," Maggie explained, her eyes dancing around the room, unable to settle anywhere, particularly not on his face. "And I know that once I'm there- Well, that home was never a happy one. I was never really... welcome in it." She dried her eyes again bitterly.

"Then don't go back," Harry said quietly.

Maggie let out a frustrated laugh and shook her head.

"What?"

"Where would I go?" Maggie said. "If I refuse to go with them, they won't let me stay here... I'll have nothing."

Harry shook his head. "Girl like you never has nothin'. Sure, you won't have all this, but you could find *something*."

Maggie pictured it, having a small place all her own, outside the shadow of her parent's threats. She shook her head clear. "Right now, all I care about is keeping Camila and my brother safe."

Harry straightened, eyeing her earnestly. "We will."

CHAPTER
19

MAGGIE PASSED THE MORNING of the wedding in a fugue of determination. Whatever may or may not befall her after today had been effectively banished from her thoughts, as her sole focus was set on aiding the success of the day's nuptials. The first of such duties was to get Jonathan to the church, clean, dressed, and in a fit mental state to stand before hundreds of guests and make his marriage vows. Maggie had arrived early that morning at the apartment to do just that.

This proved to be a more trying task than she had anticipated once set alongside the long list of chores set before her as the maid of honor. Jonathan moved about the apartment in a cloud of agitated energy, redoing tasks (incorrectly), misplacing important trinkets, and listing out useless instructions to Maggie each time he caught sight of her.

"When we get to the church, I'll need you to check in with the kitchen. The baker seemed behind task the other day," Jonathan blustered as he emerged from his rooms again. "It seems it may be unusually hot outside. Do you suppose? I would hate for the icing to melt."

"I do believe they account for such things," Maggie said, checking her carefully pinned curls in the mirror. They were done in tight ringlets and held up in what deceptively appeared to be an effortless heap. It was anything but. "I'll check in on it first thing. If there's any damage, I'll have them right it."

Jonathan nodded briskly.

She had personally promised to see to each and every one of his concerns, even though all issues of the kitchens fell under Mrs. Huddleston's purview. However, Maggie's duties involved ensuring that all persons of the wedding party were properly dressed and handled.

Satisfied with her own appearance, Maggie turned from the mirror. She wasn't dressed yet in her gown for the ceremony and wouldn't bother until she arrived at the church. It was packed away in a garment bag now draped over the settee. Maggie looked through the case beside it, ensuring that all the essential supplies were included within. It was all there. She had made sure of that the night before, but it was still a comfort to see it all laid out, nonetheless.

"Maggie-" Jonathan said rather abruptly behind her. She whirled around, clutching her chest with undue distress. He looked at her strangely. "Are you alright?"

Maggie let out a breath and relaxed. "It's just the morning." She waved him off.

His eyes were practically brimming with thoughts, but none escaped him.

"I'm fine, Jonathan," Maggie said stiffly. "Today is about you and Camila."

He drew in a long breath. "It's just- Well, I'm going to miss... having you here."

Maggie looked back at him in surprise.

He gave her a vulnerable glance but pressed on. "The year I was here on my own, before you came... Well, it was terribly lonely. I must confess I was somewhat selfish in interceding with Mother and Father for you to move to the city. At first, I regretted it," Jonathan laughed, and Maggie could not help but snort. "But I feel in some ways I lost you when I went off to school. These last two years... Well, I'm glad to have had them."

Maggie nodded tearfully. As much of a nuisance as they often found one another, Maggie was thankful too and was equally devastated that it was coming to an end. But she couldn't say that to him. Especially not today. So instead, she said, "You're going to love the next days even better, with Camila... starting a family."

Instead of smiling, he just looked at her with a guilty expression. It was obvious what he was thinking. Her next days were certainly not going to be *even better*. But she wouldn't have him feeling an ounce of guilt today. So, Maggie smiled through the ache and turned back to rummaging through her case.

"Make sure your bag is packed," she said over her shoulder. "The car will be here at a quarter till."

The next hour slipped by without a moment's time to breathe. After they'd loaded everything into the car, there was a bit of a fiasco on the way to the church. Jonathan insisted he had left his shoes at the apartment, and they needed to turn back. After he went to scour the apartment, Maggie found them packed in the bottom of the wrong case in the car. This delay set them far enough behind their scheduled arrival time at the church that as soon as they entered, Maggie and Jonathan ran their own separate ways without so much as a word to the other. She set her course directly to the bridal dressing suite.

"Oh, Margaret, there you are!" Camila's mother's voice rang down the hall.

Maggie halted in her tracks and turned reluctantly. Her arms were overburdened with three garment bags, two cases, and a hatbox. Nevertheless, she said gracefully, "Yes, Mrs. Huddleston. Is there something you need?"

"My mother-in-law has just arrived, and I'm sure that it was not intentional-" Her subtle sour expression suggested she was sure it had been. "-but your mother seems to have seated her three rows behind the altar. Her hearing is not as it used to be. Something will have to be done."

"Of course," Maggie said, unsurprised in the least that her mother would attempt these last minute slights. "The first row is reserved for the flower girls. Why doesn't she move there to the front and keep them company?"

Mrs. Huddleston nodded contently.

"Jonathan was anxious this morning about the cake," Maggie said, beginning to walk down the hall again. Mrs. Huddleston kept her pace.

"It's already arrived and looks fabulous," she said, nodding. "No nuts either, I made sure."

Maggie smiled and offered her thanks before they parted ways.

"Maggie!" Camila exclaimed as she entered the bridal ready room. Her other bridesmaids had already arrived, along with her two sisters, who would be acting as flower girls. "Thank goodness you're here. How is Jonathan?"

"Very much in love with you," Maggie said with a smile as she set down her load on the table. "Everything is absolutely as it should be."

Maggie stood straighter and let out a tight breath. No one was dressed yet, though there would be time for that. They would do the young girls last, Maggie decided, so they wouldn't risk tearing or dirtying their gowns. The bridesmaids were still working on their own hair, but Camila's was utterly perfect. Everything really was as it should be...

An anxious feeling came over her. A cool sensation spreading over her skin as, for the first time all morning, Maggie allowed her fears to creep over her. The police had not yet managed to apprehend Howard Towlson, a fact that she had confirmed that morning. She had not allowed this unsettling fact to distract her through the hectic morning. But now that matters were more settled, she needed to find Harry.

Maggie made an excuse to leave, which she immediately forgot. Camila didn't seem to be paying too much attention anyhow, absorbed by her own cloud of nervous energy.

"Oh, Maggie, can you find my father?" Camila asked, as she was almost out the door. "I'd like to talk to him before the ceremony."

"I'll bring him back with me," she agreed.

Maggie combed the halls. They were empty except for a few ushers dashing to complete their own tasks. The sanctuary, however, was bustling with activity as the flowers were arranged along the pews and on the altar. She stopped a moment to make sure everything was in order and turned with a satisfied nod. As she hurried through the grand double doors at the end of the aisle, Maggie nearly collided into a man standing just on the other side.

"Pardon me," Maggie said reflexively as she rebounded several steps.

Harry turned, his dark auburn hair combed and oiled back, framing his face along with the high collar of his suit. It was a sight to behold. He was handsome, to say the least, polished up this way, but it was still a bizarre change from his usual rugged appearance. She wondered where he'd managed to find the suit. It certainly wasn't the height of fashion, but it was leagues of difference from what he'd been wearing the other day. She caught herself staring rather shamelessly when his jaw set in a familiar way, and he crossed his arms, creasing his jacket sleeves unforgivingly.

Maggie couldn't help but smirk.

"I don't like this," he said under his breath. For a moment, she thought he was referring to his new attire, but then she followed his gaze, surveying the building. "Too many ways in, too many places to hide."

Uneasiness gripped her as well, but she took a deep breath. "We just need to make sure Camila is safe," Maggie said. "Her dressing room is just down there." She pointed down the hall from where she'd come.

Harry nodded. "What about your brother?"

Maggie bit her lip. This was a nightmare. She had hoped that the police would find Howard before today, but by all accounts, it seemed that New York's finest had been chasing nothing but their tails for three days.

"Is there a way you could, you know, find him?" he asked.

"Find him?" Maggie repeated.

"Well, you knew his name, what he looked like, couldn't you just..." he let out a frustrated breath. "I don't understand whatever it is you do, but you could try lookin' for him."

Maggie shook her head. "That's not how it works. I'm not a psychic. I only talk to the dead."

He huffed, disappointed, as a florist walked past with another armload of peonies.

"I'm supposed to find Camila's father."

Harry nodded. "I'll keep an eye on her."

"What if someone asks-"

He raised his brow. "I'll blend in, eh?" Then he turned down the hall.

Maggie's hands shook faintly as she made her way toward the opposite side of the church where Jonathan and his groomsmen were preparing. She thought perhaps that Camila's father might be among them. It was possible, she supposed, but mostly, she needed to see that her brother was safe. The chances of the killer being here were small, Maggie tried to assure herself. There was still a chance that he had fled the city. He could be a hundred miles away by now.

Inside the dressing room, she could hear the muffled sounds of male conversation and laughter. At least that boded well. Maggie knocked loudly.

"Jonathan!"

It was quiet for a moment before the doorknob turned and her brother emerged. He was dressed in his wedding suit, well half dressed. Only half of the buttons were done, his tie slack around his neck. "Is something wrong?" he asked at once.

"No, no," Maggie dismissed quickly. "I'm looking for Mr. Huddleston. Have you seen him?"

Jonathan shook his head. "How is Camila?"

"Perfect," Maggie said, forcing a smile. If she had her way, they would never know the fear charging through her at this very moment. This day would be perfect for them if it killed her.

Her brother nodded approvingly and then huffed in such a way she could only ask, "What's wrong?"

His expression soured further. "I left a gift in Camila's ready room last night, a clock," Jonathan explained, his hands coming to settle on his hips. "Someone brought it in here and- It's utterly ruined."

"They broke it?" Maggie asked.

He shook his head sharply. "They destroyed it. The damage was rather beyond an accident. It seems it was dropped, and then a boot was taken to it. I can't understand who would do such a thing!"

Her brother continued to complain about how he would be contacting the church management. He was sure this was some ill tasted prank of the ushers or even a break in. Maggie was barely listening. She had to tell Harry. Now. It was too much of a coincidence not to be a threat against her brother. Ice settled in her veins. If Howard had been here last night to destroy the clock... He could be here even now...

"Jonathan," Maggie said suddenly, certain she was interrupting. "It's terrible what happened, but we must move forward, right?"

He grimaced.

"Camila will never know the difference," she assured, even as her heart hammered against her chest. "Now go and get yourself dressed. She won't forgive you if you're late."

Jonathan had opened his mouth to say more, but Maggie turned and rushed down the hall. Harry would be outside Camila's room. All she had to do was follow the hall that curved behind the sanctuary to the other side of the church. It took all her self control not to run as her mind sped. Had she made a mistake leaving Jonathan alone? Was it possible she overreacting to nothing? What would Harry-

As Maggie rounded the corner to the narrow hall behind the sanctuary, everything stopped. Her heart, her breath, her thoughts. She was locked within a body that would not budge. Terror filled her so completely that she was afraid she might burst. He was standing right there. That face, long and squared, the round eyes and large nose, unmistakable. Howard Towlson, The Valentine Ripper. Not in a memory or a dream, in the flesh and alone, with her in this narrow hall.

His blonde hair was combed neatly. He was wearing an aged suit, the color faded, yet one could easily mistake him for any one of the guests who had been invited. She needed to be calm, to just turn the other way like he was a stranger and carry on her way...

but it was too late for that. He was studying her, her gaping expression, the color draining from her face. Howard's eyes narrowed. His demeanor changed, angling toward her.

RUN! Her mind pleaded. Scream! Run! Anything! But it was as if the connection from her mind to her body had been severed.

In the breadth of a heartbeat, he was in motion. Maggie managed only a stumbling step backward, a strangled gasp, before he was upon her. A familiar, steely grip latched around her arm as his other hand pressed into her face. A second later, she was slammed into the wall behind her.

Desperate rage filled her as her body awoke, thrashing violently against him. This wasn't the end. Not for her. Not today. She just had to hold him off until someone found them. Maggie took in a breath. If she screamed, someone would-

His hand reeled back and slammed her head into the wall.

Light flashed in her vision, the color of pain, as it split through her skull. Beneath her, Maggie's knees buckled. Her surroundings became murky and confused as a terrible sense of unsteadiness washed over her. The ground shifted so constantly that Maggie thought she might be sick. Her eyes clenched shut to block out the world as it spun around her. There was a lurch. The sensation was confusing at first, but then clarity found her. She was being pulled, moved. This was wrong. She should fight...

But her mind was still spinning. It was darker now, wherever they were. Her feet were perpetually staggering beneath her over the uneven ground. The air was musty and stale. How had they even gotten there? Maggie struggled, her movements chaotic and feeble. His arm around her waist might as well have been an iron bar. Yet she didn't relent until, without warning, Maggie fell harshly to the ground.

CHAPTER

20

WITH LITTLE MORE THAN AN HOUR remaining until the ceremony, the church was in a state of preparatory chaos. Jonathan was in his ready room, worrying over the state of his tie and pestering his groomsmen with pointless errands to ensure everything was going smoothly. Camila, now entirely dressed, was trying to convince her two young sisters to sit still long enough for the bridesmaids to braid their hair. Meanwhile, Harry was checking the hallway for disused service passages. His exploration of his childhood parish had led him to discover many such secret rooms and narrow halls. Often these would lead to the church attic or even the exterior. He did not like the idea of masked points of entry leading to an ambush...

Maggie was lying on a dusty wooden floor. The air around her was swelteringly hot. She recalled falling to the floor. But how long ago had that been? Her every thought swam through a thick and muddled haze. The ringing in her ears persisted. She hadn't dared open her eyes. Had she lost consciousness? Was Howard- Was he still there?

Heavy footfalls creaking against the floor gave her answer enough. Maggie listened for a moment. The footsteps sounded in one direction, only to turn back and trace the same path. He was pacing. Obviously, he hadn't meant to run into her, to be recognised. Her heart quickened. That meant she was entirely dispensable, the perfect target for his frustrations.

Maggie tried to push down the steady tide of fear. She couldn't let it overwhelm her again. What she needed was a plan, and lying on the floor playing unconscious was hardly going to solve anything. They were still in the church. She was almost certain of that. Which meant that she would not have to get far. A quick distraction and sprint may even be enough. The floor tilted sickeningly beneath her at even the thought of standing. Running may not even be an option.

What was left? To scream? He could get violent... She may not last until help came, supposing they could hear her at all. To fight? That was a laughable thought. Perhaps if she had her brother's gun- Then the answer hit her. She didn't need to physically overpower him. She didn't need a gun.

Maggie just had to touch him...

Her eyes opened a crack, soaking in every detail of the space as quickly as possible, even as her vision whirled and slanted. Faint light filtered through a grimy stained glass window on the far wall.

They were still in the church, and that must be the direction of the street. There were many crates and covered furniture. A large bell stood blanketed in dust in the corner. The ceiling was high, the exposed beams coming to a point. The church attic.

Howard was still pacing, only a few feet away from her motionless body. Beyond him, she could see what looked like a makeshift bed. There were bags of supplies as well, clothes, random food items. He'd been living up here... For how long?

As she watched him, two more details fell heavily upon her. Firstly, he was muttering to himself, words unintelligible to her, and more pressingly, he was holding a knife. A knife she recognised. A chill came over her skin at the sight of it, the touch of the void. The mist caressed her as if it shared in her outrage... as if they were allies... of one mind... She had felt this way once before, when her life had been in peril. Anne had come to her aid. Not for her sake, of course, but for Charles, to spare him. Maggie reached out enough to recognise their voices. Katherine, Ivy, Eileen... and another. It must be Mary, she realised.

Courage filled her chest, a relieving fire against the tense chill of terror. She was not powerless, and she was decidedly not alone. They were with her, watching.

Maggie shifted her weight unconsciously and his attention came to her at once. Howard stepped closer, making a show of the knife as he crouched down just beyond her reach.

"How do you know me?" he demanded. Ordinarily, Maggie would never have been frightened of this man. He was not terribly strong and seemed to have a rather nervous disposition, but his eyes- They were desperate, unhinged, dangerous.

"The police are here. They are looking for you," Maggie lied.

His eyes began shifting at once, hands flexing and releasing. She'd seen that in the memories, the motion as he gripped and regripped the dagger. Maggie remained completely still. She couldn't help the icy rush of fear which coursed through her, even as the whispers rang in her ears. Would she soon join them?

Maggie bit down on her cheek, the pain bringing her focus back to this moment. She had to think. He must have had an escape plan. She wanted him to use it. He must feel some sense of self preservation, right? Or was he too far gone? All she knew was that she needed to get him as far from this wedding as possible... And if he tried to take her with him, she'd have a better chance of getting the upper hand.

"No, no, no," he began muttering under his breath. "She can't do this. She can't-" Howard shot up suddenly and toppled a stack of crates landing only feet away from her. The contents shattered, the remnants of glass blown ornaments and packing hay spilling over the ground.

Maggie sat up fully, propping herself up on her hands. With every subtle motion, it felt as though the floor were oscillating beneath her. Her eyes squeezed shut, but even in the darkness, her head spun violently. She peeled them open. She had to find her balance, to stay alert, to think.

"He's wrong for her. He doesn't know her! I know her!" he ranted, jabbing his fingers into his chest in emphasis. "She loved me before he came. Camila loved me. He stole her. She can't do this. She can't-" He let out a furious noise and kicked the toppled crates.

She flinched at the sound of every impact. A fear dawned within her that the more his rage grew, the more likely he was to turn it on her. "Howard," Maggie said calmly. "You've got to think. What's next? You can't stay here. The police-"

"Quiet!" he snapped, turning on her abruptly. Maggie fell silent as he turned his full attention toward her.

She should have kept her mouth shut.

"You," he said, pointing to her with the knife. "You'll take me to her. Camila will listen to you. Then she'll see me. You'll tell her that she has to see me."

There was no way on god's earth Maggie would ever do that. Resolve thundered through her. She would tackle him right here in this dusty attic before she let Camila lay one eye on him. This danger, this fear, this was Maggie's life, not Camila's. She could be haunted, as long as they could be happy.

But her chances would be better if she got out of this attic... If she could get outside... If she could find Harry somehow...

"Of course," Maggie said. "I'll take you to her. I will."

He nodded impatiently, and Maggie began to stand slowly. "She doesn't want this," Howard insisted, though it seemed he was addressing himself more than her. "She just needs to see me. She needs to know that I'm here."

The moment Maggie was remotely on her feet, he lunged forward, still fuming, clamping his hand around her arm and yanking as if she was nothing more than a rag doll. Maggie stumbled, but found her footing at his side as he led her to a set of stairs. She had no idea where they led, no inkling if they held a chance of her escape. There was only a second to make the choice, to gamble or to make her stand.

Maggie planted her feet and dug her nails into the arm that held her in a steely grip. This ended here. Not another step. Aberrant rage filled her, and she was not afraid. Shock filled his pale eyes as he felt the first whispers of the void. His other hand came to grip her hair in a tight fist. The pain was nearly blinding against the pounding bruise on the back of her skull. Tears filled her eyes until his face was swimming before her. Maggie clenched her eyes shut. Her jaw tightened until her teeth threatened to crack under the pressure as she dragged him down into the abysmal depths.

The pain dissipated. Had he let go, or was she removed enough from her body that she no longer felt it? It was impossible to say. Her focus was on his spirit struggling in her grasp. This time, she wouldn't let go. Maggie sank her claws in, deep and merciless. The cold was nothing compared to her wrath. The darkness filled with the whispers of her allies. She heard them all:

Katherine Read, Mary Foster, Ivy Shutler, Eileen Whitcher. They sang to her in one voice, triumph and sorrow.

Maggie embraced them all.

She struggled for air as Ivy fought for her life. She felt the impact of the knife as Katherine bled into the snow. Her heart nearly burst with fear as Mary never stopped trying to scream, to be seen. Sadness swelled within her for Eileen's poor peaceful spirit, who longed only for contentment, who suffered so much before peace finally came.

Maggie endured it all and bore witness to what would never be forgiven nor forgotten, because she knew he felt it too. Howard suffered through their every memory. He experienced their fear, their screams, their pain as his own. Maggie forced him to watch his own face twisted in malice, to confront the monster he was.

It was not enough punishment for his soul, but it was a start.

When it was over, Maggie released his spirit from her grasp. She could hold on no longer. Overwhelming fatigue filled her as his spirit left her for that other place, the place of light and warmth. Yet she lingered. Her veins were ice. Her heart beat a slow and solemn rhythm. She was so weary, but this was a place of rest. The darkness filled her mind with its whispers until she could think of nothing else.

And there was only darkness.

Emptiness.

Void.

.

.

.

Sunrise found her. Not soft and waxing, but harsh and sudden and calling. Warmth that thawed her heart to beat furiously in her chest. Light that brought her back to her own body which she had thought lost. In fact, she had not thought of it at all, but now she was going to collide with it. For a moment, Maggie was afraid. She wasn't ready. The warmth, the light, it was too much all at once. She had to go back, but the pull was too strong.

Maggie surfaced, screaming. The very sound was an assault to her ears.

"Maggie!" Harry's voice was a desperate growl.

His hands were gripping her shoulders, shaking her. Maggie could only make out his shape at first. The stained glass window shone behind, silhouetting him in a rainbow of light. The details came to her slowly.

"Maggie, are ya with me?" His hand moved to pat her cheek. Panic was etched into his every feature, radiating from his wide blue eyes as they darted over her face.

She shook her head against his touch, the cry fading to a groan in her throat.

"I've got you. I've got you," Harry said quickly. "Are ya hurt?"

Maggie jerked up, wincing immediately at the pain in her head. "Where is he?" she demanded, scouring the attic until her eyes fell on Howard's body only feet away from her. He lay on his stomach, utterly unconscious, his hands bound by handcuffs behind his back.

"He's not going anywhere," Harry said, echoing every ounce of bitter triumph she felt seeing him there, powerless and prone. He turned back to her, expression softening. "Are ya hurt?"

Her head pounded. The bruise continued to throb angrily at the back of her scalp. "I'll be fine," Maggie said, rubbing her brow as she sat up under her own power.

"I should have found him first," Harry said, looking at him again bitterly. "Shouldn't have left you. You were- You were-" He rubbed a hand over his mouth.

Maggie shook her head. "It's my fault. I saw him and I froze. He knew that I recognised him… I didn't even run."

"How did you…" His gaze flickered over to Howard's unconscious form.

"I showed him what he'd done," Maggie said bitterly. "I made him live through every minute of it."

His brows knotted. She waited for him to look at her in fear, to be disgusted by what she could do, but it never came. At last, all he said was, "You were barely breathin' when I found you. I thought- I thought you were…"

"I took it too far. I got lost…" she explained slowly, still becoming accustomed to her surroundings. There was simply so much to see, to smell, to feel. Had it only been moments since she'd left this place?

"And I brought you back?" Harry said, posing it as a question.

Maggie only nodded.

He mulled this over. "You need to be more careful, Maggie. Messin' with death the way you do... You've got to have someone-Someone to bring you back."

Before she could think of what to say, she heard it. The thundering sound surrounded them, paralysing her in fright. It was loud enough to feel its vibrations on the wooden floor. It took several panicked breaths for her to place it. The organ. Her eyes grew huge with realisation.

"I have to go!" Maggie said, struggling to her feet. "The guests will be arriving. He can't be here. They can't know that we found him here!"

As she stood, her balance lurched. Harry caught her before she collapsed back to the ground.

Maggie clutched her head, steadying herself before nodding to Harry.

He released her tentatively. "You need a doctor."

"No, I just stood too quickly," Maggie insisted. "I need to get down there."

Harry considered her for a moment before relenting. "I will handle him. Just do what you have to."

She nodded, going to the stairs as she tried to put out of her head how Harry was going to get Howard's unconscious body out of the church unseen. Maggie rushed as well as she could, balancing against the wall when needed. When she emerged from the unfinished wooden staircase, the air was so cool and fresh she could help but take it deep into her lungs. It was a moment collecting her bearings before Maggie realised that this was the very hall where she'd encountered Howard in the first place. She must have found him just as he'd emerged...

She took down the hall at as fast a pace as possible as the organ continued to play, roaring in her aching head.

"Maggie!" Camila's gasp was both relieved and irate as Maggie burst through the dressing room door. She was dressed in her gown. The creamy silk cascaded over her figure perfectly, the strands of pearls draping over her bodice. Her long train had been carefully laid out behind her. The other bridesmaids were just applying her veil as Camila turned to greet her. Her brown eyes examined her, making Maggie consider her own disheveled appearance for the first time.

"Camila, I'm so-" Maggie began.

The bride waved her gloved hand and shook her head. "There isn't time. Just sit. We can fix this."

Maggie sat obediently as one of the bridesmaids began to fix her hair. She bit the inside of her cheek to keep from hissing in pain every time her hair pulled against her bruise. Within ten minutes, she was presentable enough and her lavender dress was on without a crease.

Not a second later, Camila's young sisters burst into the room with their mother behind them. Their hair, which had once been brushed and braided, was now in a state of disarray. And more, the younger had a tear in the hem of her dress. Suddenly, the ready room was again swept up in a panic. Mrs. Huddleston mended the

hem at a lightning pace as Maggie and Camila's cousin, Deborah, retamed the girls' wild hair.

"How's everything?" Camila asked her mother nervously.

"Everything is going perfectly," Mrs. Huddleston answered. "Everyone is simply waiting for you."

Camila looked at her, warm cheeks draining of color.

"You've been planning for this, remember?" Maggie reassured.

"Yes," Camila said, standing up straighter and looking at herself in the tall mirror against the wall. She began to pick at her hair and dress, straightening everything anxiously.

"You look wonderful. Everything is going smoothly, and it will all be over soon," her mother soothed, looking on at her reflection with loving eyes.

As Maggie set the last braid, an usher knocked on the door. Camila's eyes widened as they all scurried about in a final madness.

"My bouquet?" Camila called as her bridesmaids whisked her out of the door with her veil and train in hand.

"I have it here!" Maggie called, holding it in hand with her own.

Mr. Huddleston was waiting for them outside as they formed hurriedly into their lines. Maggie took her place behind the other bridesmaids as Mrs. Huddleston put the girls in order behind her. As they began to march forward toward the sanctuary, Maggie turned to give Camila a reassuring smile. Camila was taking quick panicked breaths, though a broad smile had stretched across her face.

Soon they were stepping forward to the sound of the organ until the aisle was before them. The large church was filled with guests, most of which Maggie didn't recognise, even on her own family's side. She couldn't help but to scan the crowd until she laid eyes on her brother at the end of the aisle. However, his gaze was firmly locked on his bride making her way toward him as if she were a heavenly sight.

CHAPTER

21

THE CEREMONY HAD GONE ON without incident, beautifully sentimental and wonderfully romantic. Maggie's head had pounded the entire time. Yet, it was worth it. Everything was worth it, seeing the freshly wedded bliss that surrounded the pair as they led the precessional back down the aisle. They had gone from there to the reception at The Plaza. Maggie had been stuffed into a car between her parents and George, surviving their conversation with a series of noncommittal sounds and vague half answers. It was the best she could manage. Through her blinding headache, there was only so much room for thought. That precious focus was centered entirely on the events of that morning.

Maggie had not seen a hint of Harry, nor heard the sound of police sirens outside. Not a single disturbance. Worry had sprouted in her once or twice that Howard might have overpowered Harry and escaped. It was not as if she had been able to go back to the attic to check. But Maggie pushed those doubts from her mind. In the state she'd left him, he wouldn't have been capable of any such thing.

In the ballroom of The Plaza, there were luxuries abounding. The hall itself was flanked by thick column sentries that supported the Parisian moldings decorating the ceiling. Surveying the grandeur from above were a number of crystal chandeliers. Tables overflowed with delicious food and sweet smelling flowers. Fine wines and champagne flowed festive and freely. Happiness hung in the air like a euphoric mist that seemed to radiate from the newlyweds. In the midst this overwhelming joy, Maggie began to drink, soothing the still throbbing ache in her skull.

On her first glass of champagne, she was content to pay mild attention to the speeches in tribute to her brother and new sister-in-law. It did ease the pain well enough, and her worries too. By the second, however, she was paying no attention whatsoever to the speakers. Maggie had been seated with the other bridesmaids and groomsmen, for which she was rather grateful. In her living memory, she had never wanted to avoid her parents more than she did that day. Any delay of the inevitable conversation of her moving back home in the coming days was desirable, to say the least.

Maggie was halfway through her third champagne, and beginning to feel it in her head, when the toasts were finally over. She had it in her mind to sneak off somewhere. Doubtlessly, her parents were preparing at this very moment to ambush her. If she could only find some secluded, quiet corner... Maggie stood, tripping over the leg of her chair.

"Margaret!" a voice said, startled as she nearly knocked into him.

"Oh, my apologies," Maggie said, looking up to see George. It was hard to mask a grimace at being foiled so quickly.

"I was just looking for you. Are you alright?" he asked.

"Fine, yes," Maggie said, fixing a loose curl of her hair.

"In that case, could I talk to you about a private matter?"

Maggie looked at him blankly, wishing to God she could simply say no and walk away. "Of course," she sighed and followed him out to the edges of the ballroom.

They came to a stop behind one of the thick pillars. George looked at her, as though for once he was having sincere difficulty finding words.

"Margaret," George began as Maggie took a preparatory sip. "I feel I must begin by saying that I am aware of your situation and how delicate it is. I have spoken with your parents, and I know what they have set before you after today." He paused, studying her face. Perhaps he was looking for a glimmer of direction. Maggie couldn't begin to speculate what he saw there. "I rather hoped over the past months that we would have seen more of each other, perhaps become closer... But I will be returning to my post in the British Navy in a matter of weeks. There may not be time to prepare for an event so grand as this one. Perhaps we could have a larger celebration at my family home when the Great War is over."

He glanced at his hands and cleared his throat. "Until then, I could rent you an apartment here in the city. I know how much you love it here. I also know that this is very much for you to consider, but I hope…"

"George," Maggie said, stopping him from going any further. She was not surprised by the proposal, not in the least. What had taken her utterly by surprise was how tempting it sounded. Freedom to remain in the city, a wealthy husband on the other side of an ocean… But for how long?

George straightened, hearing the refusal in her tone.

"That sounds like a perfectly wonderful life," she eased, "living in luxury, needs met, with a man who I certainly respect and may even grow to care for, but George… I do not want a life that is easy. I want a life that is my own. I want to make my own choices unburdened by the will of others. I cannot marry now just to please my parents, whatever the outcome may be. I cannot."

"I see," he said, rubbing his chin. "You are kind to let a man down so gently, and I hope that you find whatever future it is that you aim for."

"That means very much to me," Maggie said sincerely. "I know this is terribly out of line, but may I make a suggestion regarding your estate?"

George's brow furrowed, but he nodded all the same.

"You have spoken of your care for your sister, and your fears for her as well as your estate should the worst occur-" He nodded even as his brows knitted tighter together. "But have you considered that perhaps the solution to this matter hides within the issue itself?"

"How so?"

"Leave the estate to your sister, in your will, put the property in her name. You will know that she is cared for because she will certainly have the means to care for herself, and your estate will have its natural successor."

George raised his brow as he contemplated her words. "You have given me very much to consider, Ms. Ward."

Maggie nodded

"I think I will find myself another glass of that champagne." He departed with a stiff smile, disappearing into the crowded ballroom.

Maggie drained the last of her glass in one gulp, but did not take another. Her head was swimming enough as it was. Her sobered mind wanted to contemplate the implications of what she had just done, the consequences which would surely rain down on her the moment her mother learned of what had happened, but it was drowned beneath three glasses of champagne.

As Maggie stationed herself on the outskirts of the dance floor, her thoughts turned instead to Charles. It seemed almost inevitable as she thought about it... How could she not compare this to a similar evening? He had found her like this, standing alone... She'd been lost then, even in a room full of people, but he had found her. He had helped her find herself again. The kiss they shared that night haunted her now, taunting her dreams with bliss, only to fill her waking hours with longing. Now what she wouldn't give just to stand beside him, just to hear his voice… Her wanting was so strong, Maggie could have sworn that for a single moment she sensed his presence behind her. A faint scent in the air, a shadow in the corner of her eye. The madness swept her up enough to even look over her shoulder.

No one. Nothing but the conjuration of a lonely mind. A tear trailed down her cheek before she had even realised it had escaped. Maggie whisked it away with her gloved hand.

She had to write him back, Maggie decided then. No matter what happened in these uncertain days ahead. She had to let Charles know… that she would be here when he returned. That he must return. He needed to know how terrified she was… that he wasn't forgotten. Perhaps her silence these weeks had been punishment for leaving her a second time, for putting her in this place of perpetual worry. She was not sure that she had forgiven him for that. No, in fact, she had not. But he had to know that-

Maggie cut off her own thoughts with a shake of her head, turning abruptly to the bar. Even as she cut through the crowd, another betraying tear slid from her eyes. She wiped it away quickly and composed herself. One can only allow so much self punishment in a single day. Any more and she would be liable to crumble here and now, an unacceptable eventuality.

"Whiskey, please," Maggie said clearly to the bartender.

He eyed her, his own opinions written plainly in his expression, but Maggie stared him down fiercely. Soon he was sliding the glass down the polished bar. Maggie took a long sip and sighed as it burned down her throat.

"Lighten up, lass. It's a wedding, not a funeral," Harry's voice sounded beside her.

Maggie chose to ignore his comment as she turned to him with far more pressing concerns on her mind. "Is everything managed?" she asked.

He nodded once as he leaned his elbows against the bar. He was still wearing the same suit as that morning, though it was decidedly more wrinkled than before. "I'll have what the lady's having," he told the bartender, who responded with a short nod.

"Why did you come back?" Maggie asked. "I wasn't expecting to see you."

"The station has everything handled well enough without me," Harry said. The bartender set the glass before him and he took his first sip. "Damn, that's good." He drank again. "I came to check up on you, but I think I will be staying for this," he said, admiring the amber liquid as it caught the light.

Maggie laughed. What started as a chuckle loosed from her wild enough to shake her sides. "I'm great," she managed as she reined in her breath once more.

"Yeah, sure ya are," Harry said with a grin. He plucked her drink from her grasp and drained the rest before putting it back in her hand.

Maggie's jaw set angrily.

"Want me to take you home?" he asked casually, ignoring her indignant glare.

Home? She didn't have a home, not anymore. The Warren Street apartment was Jonathan and Camila's place now. Her parent's house in the country had never been a home, never could be... Where was she supposed to go? And then she was crying, not single trailing tears, but gushing sobs that would not be stopped or silenced or whisked away.

"Woah, easy there." Harry closed the distance between them and put an arm around her shoulder. Whether or not it was intentional, his body masked her from the others about the ballroom.

Maggie sniffed and tried to bring herself together, but it was a futile effort as tears came in brutal waves. Instead, she buried herself into Harry's jacket as if she could just disappear into his arms.

"Let's get you out of here," Harry said quietly. Maggie nodded against his shoulder as he led her. She couldn't see where through her tears and didn't much care.

"Margaret!" Maggie winced as her mother's harsh whisper sliced through the air.

This was perhaps the singular force on earth that could have caused her relentless sobs to come to a sudden and striking halt. Maggie dried her tears as she turned to see her mother coming toward them. To the casual observer, Mrs. Ward may have seemed a proper, collected lady, but Maggie could see the steam pouring from her nostrils like an enraged bull. Harry withdrew his arm as Maggie turned, a motion which her mother watched with cold, calculating eyes.

"Would you like to explain the conversation I have just had with Mr. Cromwell?" she hissed.

"How am I to know what you discussed?" Maggie said haughtily, though her throat was still betrayingly tight, her eyelashes still wet with tears.

"You know very well what I'm talking about," Mrs. Ward said, every word sharp enough to cut. "I expect you to apologise to him, tomorrow, and accept his offer. Now you need to go upstairs. Collect yourself at once. You reek of drink. I won't have you embarrassing your brother or this family any further."

"I have nothing to apologise for," Maggie said. "I gave him my answer. It's finished."

"Why must you punish me like this? Marrying George is a good match. I simply don't understand why you are being so unreasonable," Mrs. Ward lamented. "It's clear to me now that we should have never let you come to the city. Look at you! You've forgotten everything we've taught you. It was a miracle that Mr. Cromwell was interested in seeking a proposal at all. And your brother's supervision was clearly not enough if this is the sort of company you're keeping."

It took a moment for her words to sink in as her mother's eyes never fell on Harry at her side, but clearly her strike had been directed toward him. She chanced only a brief look up at Harry's hardened expression, his jaw set tensed and angry beneath his cheek.

"Good night, Mother," Maggie said with every ounce of venom she possessed. Her eyes did not waver as she linked her arm with Harry's. It took only a small nudge before he understood her intention and began steering her from the ballroom.

Though she could nearly feel the billowing rage spilling from her mother, she made no move to stop them. It tasted like victory, however short Maggie knew it would be. Her parents' retribution was always a swift and forceful thing.

"Delightful mother you've got there," Harry said as they came to the hall. His tone was still biting.

Maggie grimaced. "Not in the slightest." She steered them toward the elevators. She needed somewhere quiet to think, to stop the pounding in her head.

The gate shut, and the operator took her to the correct floor without even having to ask her name.

"So, George?" Harry said as the doors opened. "Is he-"

Was he the man he met in the lobby the other night? "Yes," Maggie answered shortly.

"Seemed nice... rich," Harry mused.

"Exceedingly." She stepped quickly down the hall, holding her key in hand.

"Not your type?"

Maggie paused before unlocking the door, realising that he was not just trying to irk her with this line of questioning. Still, she let his question hang in the air as she turned the key and opened the door to the suite that was her own. It was smaller than her parents' but still offered a comfortable sitting area, even if it was in the same room as the bed.

Maggie nodded in invitation as she stepped inside. Her mother would lay an egg to know she had invited a man into her room, but in this moment, she was far beyond caring about her parent's wishes. Harry shut the door as she dropped the key on the little table and rubbed her temples.

"Are you still hurtin'?" he asked, rather closer to her than she had expected.

"It's just my head. I just need to rest. I haven't had a moment's peace since-"

Harry nodded sparingly. "I shouldn't have let that happen."

"You couldn't have been everywhere at once," Maggie posed.

He raised his brows in obstinate disbelief. "I knew it wasn't safe."

"So did I." She advanced on him, only to find that they had come very close indeed. His expression softened, and she recognised what lay within. The gentle concern on his brow. His eyes were set in worry, even guilt. More telling was what Maggie could see thinly veiled beneath.

Her breath caught in her throat. That's why he'd been so keen to ask about George, perhaps why he'd been so upset to see him in the lobby that night. Should she really be so surprised? He had asked her if she was romantically attached after that night at the pub. Why did it seem so impossible to her that he was looking at her this way now? As if he might reach out and kiss her, hold her, touch her… as if he had imagined doing so more than once before.

Maggie stepped back even as her cheeks flushed, her heart beating against her chest in a brutal rhythm. Harry's gaze lowered at once to the ground.

"I really should rest," Maggie said. "I'm not well."

"Of course," he nodded, still not meeting her eye. He stepped toward the door but hesitated. "Are you gonna be alright? With your family and all?"

She had no idea. "I will figure something out," Maggie managed to say with far more conviction than she felt.

He looked at her a moment longer, as though he heard through her confidence anyhow. "Your mother was wrong about you, you know. Everything she said about you not deserving a man like that. He'd have been bloody lucky to have ya, Maggie. Any guy would." Maggie stared back mutely until he nodded, dismissing himself. "Good night, Maggie."

Words filled her mouth as he turned away, though she wasn't even sure what she meant to say. But before she could sort it all out, it was too late. Harry had closed the door softly behind him, leaving only a palpable emptiness in his wake.

CHAPTER 22

MAGGIE WOKE LATE THAT MORNING, very late. The sunlight had entirely invaded her room, spilling over the inelegant heap she had created for herself in the covers. She lifted her heavy head, squinting in the light. How had such a long night passed so quickly and left her feeling so wretched in spite of it all?

A knock sounded impatiently at her door. "Ms. Ward, your family is awaiting you in the lobby."

Maggie sat up, remembering the proverbial hurricane in store for her today with a prolonged groan. Her tardiness was hardly going to make matters any easier.

"Unless you'd like to extend your stay with us another night, I must ask that you vacate the room at once, miss," the outside voice said, polite but firm.

Kicking herself free from the covers, Maggie stood. Her head swam, and she thrust a hand against the wall to keep herself from toppling over.

"Miss, are you alright in there?"

Maggie cursed as she squeezed her eyes shut, demanding her balance to right itself at once. "Perfectly well, thank you. So sorry. I must have overslept." She chanced to open her eyes again when she felt steadier on her feet and everything seemed to remain in its proper place. Maggie rushed to her luggage, neatly packed on the other side of the room. There was a large standing cabinet trunk and two smaller cases, enough clothes and essentials for the three weeks she had spent in and out of these rooms. Thankfully, only a few loose items needed tucking away.

In an anxious flurry, Maggie pinned her hair, avoiding the still angry lump at the back of her head. Sooner than she would have thought possible, she was dressed and opening the door. A stern concierge was standing just without alongside a straight backed bellhop. Maggie smiled at them both with an aggressively honeyed expression as they collected her things and joined her silently in the elevator.

As they reached the lobby, the elevator gate parted before her. As Maggie stepped out, a heaviness settled on her shoulders as it does when one is set to encounter their fate.

Her parents watched her from beneath the massive chandelier, two middle aged persons wearing the finest of traveling clothes and the sourest of expressions. As she came toward them,

Maggie almost wished that some stroke of grim luck would favor her and whatever tethered that massive crystal fascinator would grow tired and allow it to mercifully crush them all. Unfortunately, it stayed resolutely overhead, prepared to watch whatever was about to unfold below, busybody that it was.

"Our train departs at two o'clock," Mrs. Ward said, hardly looking at her daughter. Her expression was threateningly light, as if daring her to dispute a matter that was entirely settled.

"What about George?" Maggie asked, matching her mother's tone. "I thought I was meant to offer my apologies."

"Mr. Cromwell," her father said, each syllable uniquely outraged, "has already left. He said that upon reflecting that you were quite right and that the match would not have been the proper course for either of you." Clearly, her father thought otherwise.

"I'm glad he harbors no resentment," Maggie said placidly, and rather truthfully, as well.

"No resentment?" Mr. Ward sputtered the words back at her.

"You cannot carry on like this, Margaret," her mother hissed. "Another broken engagement and people will begin to wonder why."

"George and I weren't engaged, Mother," Maggie said.

By her mother's expression, it seemed that was entirely a matter of opinion. "When you return home, we will find someone for you, and this childish nonsense will end. Heaven help me, I will see it through myself," she resolved.

"You intend to drag me down the aisle, then?" she snapped back. "Is that it?"

"You will heed us," her father said in a tone so dangerous Maggie recoiled. He was not one to speak to her so harshly. In fact, never in her life did Maggie recall her father looking at her with such a severe expression. "You will cause this family no more embarrassment."

There was simply nothing that could be said to that. As such, Maggie stood there silently, small and aching.

"Jonathan," her mother crooned, looking over her shoulder. "Camila, so good to see you before you set off."

Maggie turned to see her brother and his new wife approaching from the elevator arm in arm with matching jovial smiles.

"Of course, Mother," Jonathan said, greeting her with a hug.

"Maggie?" Camila's hand on her shoulder reminded her that she wasn't, in fact, invisible. "Maggie, what's wrong?"

Around them, Mr. and Mrs. Ward stiffened. Jonathan turned to her and back to her parents. "Mother, it is entirely alright with the both of us if Margaret remains in the apartment."

"Jonathan, you must stop coddling your sister's whims," Mrs. Ward said sternly. "Your sister needs to join the real world, and clearly needs a firmer hand to do so."

"Our man is already overseeing the packing of your sister's things to meet us at the station."

"What?" Maggie said, outrage breaking through her silence.

Her parents ignored her like a troublesome child.

"This seems extreme, don't you think?" Jonathan pressed.

Their mother's eyes narrowed. Her son had never challenged her so brazenly. "The matter is not up for discussion. Your sister will be returning home with us today, as we said."

"I won't," Maggie said, her words echoing in the thumping beats of her heart. "I won't."

Mrs. Ward turned on her with a short, cruel laugh. "What will you do then? Live on the streets? You'll not see another penny from us."

"She will stay with us," Jonathan said.

"As long as you support your sister's rebellion, you'll suffer the same," Mr. Ward growled.

Her brother's face reddened. She had never seen him this way toward their parents, at odds, standing ground. It was startling.

"Jonathan, don't-" Maggie protested.

"You can stay in my apartment," Camila said, pointedly speaking only to her. "The rent is paid through the month. We'll figure out the rest later."

Mr. and Mrs. Ward glared down at her furiously. "Consider your actions carefully, dear," Mrs. Ward said with deadly precision.

What was there to consider? To return home would, with no exaggeration, be the end of her. Perhaps Camila had been right. There was simply no pleasing them... Not unless she surrendered herself completely to their vision, and then what! Would that be happiness? It would be the antithesis of freedom. The death of passion. And love? Well, that would steadily become a more remote and distant word until she forgot its meaning entirely.

For a single moment, lightness filled her before dreadful fear coiled her tight again. Discomfort, destitution, death. That's where rebellion would lead her. Without their money, she hardly had enough to support herself with only the earnings from her sittings. If even Jonathan was forbidden from helping her... Then Maggie considered Harry's words. Yes, she might not have everything she was accustomed to, but there was a far distance from the wealth she had been surrounded by her whole life and *nothing*. Perhaps she could set her sights on something in between. Besides, Maggie thought darkly, what good was money when you'd lost your soul?

"It is my life," Maggie ground out, "and I will live it." The power of her words snaked through her veins. She felt them etching into her bones, or perhaps they'd always been written there and she'd only just dared to read them.

"You are a foolish, ungrateful girl," Mrs. Ward said furiously. "You will ruin yourself." She turned from her then as cooly as if she were a disappointing stranger.

"You shame yourself and this family supporting this," Mr. Ward growled at her brother before he turned to join his wife. Maggie watched after him, trying to imagine how she had ever thought that Jonathan took after their father.

Camila's arm came around Maggie's shoulder with a comforting squeeze. "I think that was rather well done," she said softly.

Maggie's eyes wandered to her brother, who appeared completely lost in his own thoughts. The whole ordeal was beginning to feel rather surreal as her parents disappeared from sight. Had she really done this?

"I will be back shortly," Jonathan said suddenly, and took off in a purposeful stride across the lobby.

Both Maggie and Camila gaped after him in confusion. Part of her worried he was off to try to mend things, but surely he knew better.

As they waited for him to return, Camila ushered Maggie to a comfortable seat. She talked on about how Maggie had done the right thing, how she shouldn't worry, things would sort themselves out given time. It was a sentiment easily imparted by someone who knew where they would sleep tonight, whose needs were more than cared for by Jonathan's ample bank salary and her own family's wealth. It was a comfort Maggie had lived under her entire life. Now it was gone. Her wellbeing had been thrust into her own hands, an uneasy position. However, on the exchange, she now held her own future as well. That thought brought with it the first hint of ease she had felt all morning. It was a short lived feeling. She would feel the full excitement of the prospect when her future was a more certain thing.

Jonathan came back to them with a winded, though satisfied, expression.

"Well?" Camila prompted him.

"I was able to arrange for Maggie's luggage to be delivered to your apartment this afternoon."

Maggie perked up. "Really?"

"It's not much," Jonathan said.

"It's better than nothing," Maggie said bleakly.

He made an uncomfortable gesture. "We'll sort this mess out," he promised.

"Aren't the both of you due on a ship tomorrow morning?" Maggie asked, realisation dawning on her.

The couple exchanged a brief look before Camila waved her hand. "We'll have plenty of opportunity for a honeymoon later. Really, I don't think I could enjoy myself properly, not knowing if you were alright."

"She's entirely right," Jonathan added, interrupting Maggie's budding argument.

In the end, Maggie was entirely too grateful to push the matter any further.

Camila's lodging was more of a dormitory than an apartment. The single room consisted of a small bed, a sturdy wardrobe, and a writing desk. There was a heating coil beneath the small window that overlooked the street below. Meals were served downstairs, overseen by the building's matron, Mrs. Thatcher. She was a stern and busy woman who had no time for more than short, practical sentences. Her boarding house was filled with single ladies, each of them a professional of some sort.

For the first days, Maggie did her best not to interact with any of them. Not out of any kind of malice or dislike, she just simply was not in the mood for much more than sulking. The idea of striking out on her own had only grown more terrifying by the day as she considered her meager earnings from her sittings and how they would never be enough to support herself. Would she even be able to afford to remain in the city? Not to mention that she could not even open her own accounts with the bank or even sign a lease... For the first time, all her notions of suffrage and the disparity of women's rights in society became less of an ideal to be chase and more of a necessity to be demanded.

Camila had stopped by twice, alone, since men were not allowed within the building. She had assured Maggie that Jonathan was working tirelessly to *come to a solution*, whatever that meant. After some prying, Maggie had also learned that her father had written to say that he would be watching the accounts closely to ensure that Jonathan did not support his *errant sister* in any way.

After a time, Maggie began to look at the women around her who woke early in the morning in such a rush and were out until dinner. She listened as they spoke about their work in the newspaper, in offices and restaurants. One was an actress, another a teacher. She even overheard them speaking, through the incredibly thin walls, about the men they were meeting in restaurants and dancing halls. Maggie understood why Camila had enjoyed their companionship, for she had never encountered anything quite like it.

Still, after a week, Maggie was feeling thoroughly cooped up. Sitting at the breakfast table, Maggie continued her usual silence as the others chattered happily around her. Her eyes ranged curiously over the morning paper belonging to Ms. Abigail Porter, the secretary, who sat just to her left. A familiar name snagged her attention.

"Could I read this?" Maggie asked.

Abigail turned, seeming rather surprised that Maggie had spoken at all. She nodded, smiling brightly anyhow, and sliding the paper over.

On the front page, the title proclaimed: HERO OFFICER PROMOTED: GIVES EXCLUSIVE INTERVIEW. Maggie continued to read the article detailing how Officer Harry Mulligan had been promoted to the position of detective, just like his uncle, Detective Hugh Mulligan, before him. It recounted Harry's involvement in the arrest of Howard Towlson... Maggie's eyes nearly bulged out of her head as she spilled orange juice all over the tablecloth.

Detective Mulligan notes the involvement of local medium, Maggie Barlow, claiming "without her assistance, the killer would still be on the streets." Ms. Barlow has been noted to be involved in the arrest of another killer last January and has been accredited by the American Society for Psychical Research...

Maggie looked up at the table of ladies, now all looking at her in utter bewilderment. "I'm in the paper..." she said breathlessly.

"What?" Abigail said, taking the paper to see for herself

For the rest of the meal, there was talk of nothing else as the orange juice was allowed to soak into the tablecloth, forgotten. They peppered her with questions. Was she really a medium? How did she help the police? Was she going to keep working with them? Could she do a sitting here?

Thankfully, one by one, they looked panicked at the clock and had to rush off to this obligation or that. At last, only Maggie remained with only one thought in her mind; she had to see Harry.

Maggie took in a breath before she set her foot on the first step leading to the police station. Inside, it was far less crowded than it had been on her last visit. The manic atmosphere had ebbed. Maggie saw many light expressions among them. The air tasted of celebration, of relief. Maggie looked for Harry in his usual place but found it occupied by another young man who she did not recognise. Perhaps he had been moved after his promotion. Her eyes scanned the room again.

"Maggie?" his voice called from behind her, laced with mild surprise. Harry emerged from the hallway that led to the offices.

She greeted him with a somewhat nervous smile.

"Is somethin' the matter?" he asked as he came to her side. His uniform was the same as she remembered, though a golden badge had replaced the silver one on his chest,

Maggie shook her head. "You mentioned me in the paper."

"Just told them the truth of it," he said unabashedly. "Want to step out?"

"If it wouldn't be any trouble."

Harry gave her a satisfied nod and led the way out of the station. There was a park just across the way. It was lively with cheery passersby, a symptom of the perfect June weather. Even so, no one took particular notice of them as they found an unoccupied bench under the shade of a generous tree.

"Good to see you still in the city," Harry said as they sat.

"It is good to be here," she said with a sigh, meaning it entirely.

"Suppose your parents weren't too pleased to leave ya behind."

"They weren't."

Harry gave her a sideways look and a crooked smile. "I knew you'd stay."

His certainty impacted her, and Maggie found herself rather speechless.

He shifted to face her. "You find a place?"

"I have a... temporary solution," Maggie admitted, looking down at her hands. "My brother is trying to help me find something more permanent. I really don't know how. I suppose I'm too terrified to ask."

"It's got to be tough, having all that money and then... not."

Maggie laughed and shook her head. "It's not the money," she admitted. "It's the uncertainty of everything. Before everything was secured... But now so much is on my shoulders."

"You're not alone though," Harry said. "Hell, I've grown my whole life with the weight of the world on my shoulders and not much more than a penny to my name... But you can't survive that way unless you've got people around to lend a hand when times get hard. My mam's always had my uncle Hugh, ever since Pa died. Now she's got me and my sisters. Life's not something you've got to go after alone."

Maggie met his eyes for the first time. They were steady. She could see the truth in them. It was different when he spoke of surviving than to hear it from Camila or her brother. From them, it was an assurance, a comfort. But Harry, he'd actually done it. He had survived without the guarantees of familial wealth. He understood this burden that was so alien to her, both exhilarating and terrifying. For all these past days, she had been worrying about how she would make things on her own, feeling utterly isolated. But Harry was right. She was not adrift, not nearly.

"You need anything, you tell me," Harry said, placing his hand on hers.

Warmth spread over her as if the sun had usurped the shade. "Do you feel that?" Maggie said without thinking.

Harry's brow tightened as his eyes bore into her, and she knew he understood. "You're always so cold, Maggie... inside."

Maggie opened her mouth, but no words came.

"When I found you... in the attic," Harry began, studying her hand in his own, "your skin was so cold. I thought he'd-" He shook his head. "I still can't understand how your heart was still beatin'"

"It's all to do with my talents, I suppose," Maggie said, sliding her hand away.

They were quiet for a moment.

"You'll tell me if you find somewhere to stay?" Harry asked.

Maggie nodded. "I will."

Harry nodded too. "If I ever needed you, for work, I mean, would you be interested? Couldn't pay much, but you did good for this city already. You could do it again."

"Of course," Maggie nodded.

"Had a question for you," Harry said rather suddenly. "The newspaper printed that you'd been involved with an arrest before. I looked into it… Ruth Jackson. She was convicted for the murder of Anne Blackbourne, the attempted murder of Anne's husband, Charles. You were there…"

Maggie shuffled, a gesture that he did not fail to notice. "Charles was a client of mine. He came to me after Anne's death…" Maggie faltered.

Harry's blue eyes were fixed on her, waiting.

"He came to think that his house was haunted, that a spirit had murdered Anne and continued to threaten his maid, Ruthie… I promised him- I promised to help him to make his home safe again. We'd made a mistake, though. It was Anne who haunted the house. She terrorised her killer in the hopes of exposing her. In the end, the house was destroyed. Ruthie almost- If we hadn't come as quickly as we had, he might have-"

Harry nodded slowly.

"He's in France now," Maggie said, wiping a tear before it could fall. Even as images of muddy trenches and bomb flares filled her mind.

"You still care for him?"

Her heart stopped painfully in her chest. "I'm just afraid, you understand?" There were no other words she could offer.

Harry reached his arm around her and Maggie's head fell naturally on his shoulder, warmth flooding her... inside. "You're goin' to be just fine, Maggie."

"Thank you," she said, the words coming from the deepest parts of herself that needed to believe those words more than anything.

CHAPTER 23

WARREN STREET WAS TOO FAMILIAR a place to feel like a stranger, Maggie considered as her feet followed the familiar path up the steps. It had been so strange, giving the address to the cab driver and not to be going home. As she came to the door marked 320, Maggie paused, contemplating whether or not she should knock. In the end, she put the thought aside and opened the door. She had been invited, after all.

Maggie hadn't been back to the apartment since before the wedding more than a week ago now. To a stranger, it wouldn't have seemed so different, but Maggie noticed the little things. A new vase was on the entry table. The patchwork quilt draped over the settee. A new clock rested on the mantlepiece, a nicer one. However, some things had not changed at all. Jonathan was sitting in his armchair, setting down the paper as she entered. Camila looked over the back of the settee, having left Maggie's usual seat empty for her.

"Maggie," Camila greeted, sweeping her into a tight hug.

Jonathan merely looked up at her with a relieved expression.

"You said that you had news?" she said, too eager for wasting time on niceties.

Her brother cleared his throat as Maggie took a seat. Her body refused to relax itself, remaining tensed with anticipation. "I've found a way for you to acquire a considerable sum. The funds should be enough to make a sizable payment into a lease if you-"

"How-?" Maggie blurted, completely aghast. "How did you get that much?"

"Well," Jonathan said slowly. "You largely have Mr. Cromwell to thank."

"You didn't ask him for money," Maggie said, paling. As much as beggars cannot be choosers, Maggie didn't consider herself a beggar, not just yet. Her pride was still worth something to her.

"Oh no," Camila disabused. "Not at all. Nothing like that."

"I offered to sell him back the horse that he bought for you," Jonathan explained. "Since it was a gift to you, legally, Father cannot claim the profits. With Midnight's win record, his value has increased. In fact, I think we undersold him, but-"

"And it's actually enough for an apartment here, in the city?" Maggie said.

"As I was going to say," Jonathan continued with a huff, "I have looked at a few properties and I've found one on the West

Side that I rather think will do. It's hardly ideal, but with the down payment we'll be able to invest, the mortgage should be reasonable. I just wanted you to take a look before I signed anything. Of course, you will be the primary tenant, and I will cosign whatever necessary. I hope you don't mind that I've arranged all the proper paperwork to become your official accountant and opened an account for your use."

Maggie sat back against the settee, reeling. Beside her, Camila was grinning madly.

"My own apartment? Really?" Maggie said.

"Entirely yours," Camila said excitedly.

"Can we see it today?"

"Tomorrow," Jonathan nodded.

Maggie thought for a moment. "Does it have a place where I could hold my sittings?"

"Well, it wouldn't be safe to have strangers in your home, living alone as you would be," Jonathan said seriously.

"But how am I-" Maggie began hotly, but Camila interceded.

"What Jonathan is trying to say is that there is an alternative."

"What?"

Camila and Jonathan exchanged a look before he answered. "When Mother and Father had your things packed, they only took what was in your bedroom."

"They didn't-" The luck of it came over her. It was too good to be true. "They left the parlor..."

"*Your* parlor," she corrected, positively beaming. "Jonathan and I discussed it, and we want you to continue hosting your sittings upstairs."

Maggie looked at them both wide eyed.

"I could hardly work in that place again," Jonathan said dubiously.

"It will give you more reasons to visit!"

Maggie wrapped her up in a grateful hug.

Then she hugged her brother tightly as well. "Thank you."

"It's no less than I should have done," Jonathan said as they parted. "It was entirely unreasonable for them to stipulate your life like that."

It still took Maggie a moment to recover from her brother speaking that way about their parents. "Thank you," she said again, meaning it enough for a second utterance and more.

A knock sounded on the door behind them, and Maggie turned, brows furrowed.

Jonathan checked his watch. "Perfect," he said as Mrs. Doyle rounded the corner to get the door.

Walter emerged from the other side hastily. His expression was flustered in an excitable manner.

"Good of you to make it," Camila said. "Please, come in."

"Thank you," Walter said. "Thank you for the invitation."

"You invited him?" Maggie asked, looking to Jonathan.

Walter straightened his glasses. "Your brother has been keeping me informed as your situation… developed."

"Oh," Maggie managed. The sight of his usual tweed suit and worn doctor's bag was so achingly familiar that Maggie actually felt tight in the chest. How had she once considered that their partnership would be over?

"What a relief it is that it seems everything has sorted itself out," Walter said, sounding genuine and winded.

"It does seem so," her brother agreed.

"Jonathan was just telling me that I may continue using the upstairs parlor for sittings," Maggie added.

"Very good, very good." Walter nodded. "I have news of my own to share with you as well." He paused a moment, collecting himself. "I have petitioned the board of the ASPR to offer me a grant to continue the research I have been conducting during our partnership, and they have just agreed."

"Walter, that's wonderful," Maggie said.

"More wonderful than that." He cleared his throat. "The grant includes a monthly retainer for you."

"Really?" Camila gasped as Maggie gaped like a trout.

"Yes, well, I think the tipping point really was the article in the paper mentioning her and the organisation by name. It's more publicity than our organisation has ever received outside of scientific publications. Of course, Maggie will have obligations to fulfill, allowing me to join in on her appointments, occasionally coming to the offices for research purposes. They may even ask for you to speak at an event or two."

Maggie sucked in a breath, remembering that she was not indeed a fish. "Of course, yes. They will really be paying me for this?"

"You undervalue your significance to our purpose," Walter noted. "When it seemed we may lose you as an asset, it was an easy decision." He cleared his throat again. "However, I also hope that this would be an opportunity for you and I to explore your talents, understand them better. Last we spoke, you were feeling ill eased. I hope with understanding, you'll be able to better master your abilities."

Maggie nodded slowly. "Yes, of course."

This new reality took its time settling into Maggie's mind. When she returned to Camila's old room in the boarding house, it was almost impossible to believe that her afternoon had not been some fantastical daydream. Gratitude welled powerfully within her. Harry had spoken about relying on others, how she wasn't alone. But there had been more support for her than she could have ever imagined when she was still under the thumb of her parents. Camila's support and offering of her apartment had given her the confidence to sever that bond, and Maggie had not brought herself to regret that choice, not even when it seemed that she might end up on the streets when the month was out. She would have been too if not for Jonathan's efforts to put a roof over her head, and Walter's intercession with the ASPR to help her keep it there. There are simply some storms one cannot weather alone.

Maggie slept that night for once peacefully, knowing that she was very far from it.

The next day, Maggie caught her first glimpse of her new home as the cab stopped outside the West Side apartment. Jonathan accompanied her as she climbed to the second floor. From the moment Maggie stepped into the apartment, she felt transported, as if through the looking glass, into a different life. The small apartment consisted of a parlor that overlooked the street below, a windowless bedroom, the smallest kitchen Maggie had ever laid eyes on, and a lavatory. The space was already furnished. She regarded this as a pleasant surprise, since she had only three suitcases to her name. Though her excitement diminished slightly as she removed the coverings to reveal dated furniture, likely older than herself. All of it smelled rather musty and carried the phantasmal odor of cats.

Upon inquiry, Maggie learned that the previous tenant, or rather the late tenant, had been an aging widow with no familial connections to be found. The landlord was prepared to sell as is for a very reasonable price, her brother informed her.

In the end, odd smells withstanding, Maggie could find few faults with the arrangement. It was near the ASPR offices and not too long a walk through the park to Warren Street. It certainly had enough space for her alone. And for her now limited means, she was unlikely to find better in Manhattan.

Jonathan signed the papers that day. Both Jonathan and Camila insisted on being with her when she officially carried her trunks over the threshold two days later. Camila had mentioned bringing a few housewarming gifts. As they arrived to help her settle in, Maggie was more than surprised to see that Camila had brought more than she had herself. Her offering of housewarming gifts comprised mainly of clothes, enough for a proper wardrobe again, curtesy of Huddleston Textiles. There was also a china teapot and silver tea service, the old mantle clock, one of Maggie's favorite pieces of art from the Warren Street apartment, and a thick knitted blanket.

After a tearful and lengthy thank you to them both, the rest of the day had been spent uncovering the furniture, washing the dishes (during which no less than three dead mice and seven large insects were found), and replacing the linens on the sagging mattress. That, Maggie decided, would be the first thing to go. When the hour grew late, Jonathan brought them dinner, which they ate at the round dining table which only seated four. There was still much to be done, tidying and dusting. The kitchen was still half in disarray from their efforts to scour it in its entirety. But they were all tasks that could be completed in the morning.

Camila and Jonathan said their goodbyes, drawn out and tentative, as if she were leaving for a long voyage at sea, and then they were gone.

Maggie stood in the apartment alone.

Maggie stood in *her* apartment.

Maggie stood.

She could vaguely hear the other tenants of the building moving above her and beneath. The smell of the upturned dust filled her nose. Maggie turned, surveying the apartment once more. The sitting room was made up of a wood framed settee, an iron stove, and a large dusty rug which was in need of a good beating. A writing desk was positioned before the window. It was all hers now, this place, these things. They may be ugly things, but there was a sweetness in it all the same.

Try as she might to relax, Maggie soon found herself in motion once more. The dirty rug was rolled up and laid next to the door to be dealt with later. She finished in the kitchen, a task that drove her very late into the night but was satisfying enough to be well worth it. The bedroom was next. She emptied the wardrobe of clothes, which all carried a rather moldy smell, and piled them by the door as well to be disposed of. Maggie noticed a battered jewelry box on the dresser, but it was noticeably empty. Clearly, the landlord hadn't sold the property completely *as is*.

It was past midnight when Maggie sat on the wooden floor beside the trunk at the foot of the bed. The lid creaked open reluctantly and Maggie peered inside. It was packed neatly. On the top were framed pictures, decades old. Maggie took them each carefully. A man and woman together with a baby on her lap, a touch of faded rouge applied to their cheeks. A bifold of the very same couple some years later. They stood outside a farmhouse with three young boys. The three boys grown with union uniforms on their backs.

After that was a stack of letters tied with string. Maggie set them aside with the greatest care. The rest were small momentos, a pocket watch, a lace baby bonnet, a collection of children's toys. A wedding dress was carefully folded and wrapped. It was surreal to see a whole life reduced to the contents of a single trunk. A chill whispered over her fingertips as she held each item, but Maggie did not disturb them. Instead, she laid everything as it was and shut the chest again.

She sat beside it for a quiet moment. The hour was quite late, which suited her well enough as Maggie lingered deep in her thoughts with only silence for company. There was a clarity to such an hour, to think free of distraction. Her muscles were stiff by the time Maggie stood and strode out to the writing desk. Inside, it was well stocked with paper and ink. She pulled out a sheet which sang as it fluttered to the desktop. The dim light of the street lamps spilled over the page as Maggie began to write...

Dear Charles,

Acknowledgments

No great project is ever completed alone. I am so grateful for the many people who supported me and helped bring this book into the world!

A shout out to my amazing team of beta readers: Katie Baum, Anna Bowers, Evan Graham, Laura Hendricks, Eric Jenkins, Dale Pate, Holly Taylor, and Paul Turner. Your perspective and time were invaluable to this project!

I'm so grateful for the help of my first ever ARC team: Blair Senter, Erin Tonucci, Hanna Ferreira, Haley Renee Baldi, Aly Woodard, Laura Matthews, Laura Patterson, Simone Felline, Brooklyn LeNeé, and Bevin Golich for helping me spread the news!

Thank you to the 164 Kickstarter backers who helped launch this book including my patron backers: Simon Felline, Emily Rousell, Elizabeth Cox, Haelee Mitchell, Amy Hubert, Sherry Mock, Jeffery Johnson, Ruby Sutton, Krystal Hain, and Joseph Grim II. You brought this book to life!

To my business partner, best friend, and favorite barista, Zack Applewhite. Your support of my writing has lifted me higher than I ever thought I could go.

Honorable mention to my cat who must wonder why I enjoy pushing these stupid buttons so much more than petting him, but loves me anyway.